Sammy and the Monsters - College Days of Magic and Mischief

Sammy's Monster Adventures, Volume 3

Freya Jobe

Published by Freya Jobe, 2024.

This is a work of fiction. Similarities to real people, places, or events are entirely coincidental.

SAMMY AND THE MONSTERS - COLLEGE DAYS OF MAGIC AND MISCHIEF

First edition. November 3, 2024.

Copyright © 2024 Freya Jobe.

ISBN: 979-8227099785

Written by Freya Jobe.

Sammy and the Monsters: College Days of Magic and Mischief

Sammy never expected college to feel so... different. The campus was buzzing with new faces, late-night study sessions, and the thrill of independence. But even as he settled into his dorm and began this new chapter of life, there was something missing—a hint of magic, a bit of adventure, and a few familiar, monster-shaped friends.

He'd grown up with Whiffle, Munch, Blinky, Snatch, and all the others by his side. Together, they'd explored every corner of his house, created epic glittery messes, and even organized their own living room theatre shows. They were his loyal friends, his partners in mischief, and his secret keepers. But Sammy had left his childhood room behind, and with it, he thought he'd also left his magical monster friends.

Yet, as he unpacked his things and settled into his new life, strange things began to happen. A glitter trail by his door. Mysterious footprints in the hallway. An extra pillow that smelled like Whiffle's favorite blanket. Could it be?

One by one, Sammy's friends started to appear, sneaking into his college life with their unique blend of magic and mayhem. Together, they turned study sessions into invisible ink pranks, explored secret corners of campus, and even helped Sammy through his toughest classes. As Sammy navigated the challenges of growing up, his monster friends were there, reminding him that magic never truly leaves us—it simply grows with us.

This is the story of Sammy and his monsters, reunited for a new set of adventures. Because while some things may change, true friendship and a love for the extraordinary never fade.

Chapter 1: The Big Goodbye

Sammy sat cross-legged on his bedroom floor, surrounded by piles of clothes, books, and keepsakes. The room he had grown up in was now a mess of open boxes and half-packed bags. He couldn't quite believe that in just a few days, he'd be leaving for college—a whole new world away from the room he'd filled with memories and adventures.

As he folded a favorite T-shirt, he noticed a soft, familiar rustling sound coming from behind him. He turned to see Whiffle, his fluffy, wide-eyed friend, waddling over with an old scarf draped around his neck and a big smile on his face.

"Hey, Whiffle," Sammy said, smiling warmly. "Didn't think you'd let me leave without saying goodbye, did you?"

Whiffle's fur fluffed up as he hugged Sammy, his paws squeezing tight. "Goodbye? Sammy, we're here to help you pack!" he said, bouncing a little with excitement. "We couldn't let you do it alone."

As if on cue, the rest of his monster friends filed in, each with their own unique style. Munch arrived with his usual stack of snacks balanced in his arms, ready to share "essential travel treats." Blinky floated over, his glow casting a soft blue light around the room, and Snatch strolled in last, adjusting his top hat as he surveyed the mess.

"So, where do we start?" Blinky asked, glancing at the scattered belongings on the floor.

Sammy laughed, feeling a bit lighter with his friends by his side. "Well, let's start with the essentials," he said, holding up an old, slightly tattered book. "This one's been with me since we found that hidden nook in the library, remember?"

Whiffle nodded, his eyes sparkling. "Oh, I remember! You read us that story about the magical lands. I think we ended up turning the whole room into an imaginary kingdom."

Blinky gave a soft chuckle. "That was the night I invented my 'glow power spell.' Every time I turned up the glow, you said I was casting a magical light."

Sammy gently placed the book in a box labelled "Memories," knowing he'd be taking a little piece of their shared history with him.

As they continued packing, Munch started picking through a pile of Sammy's clothes, tossing in a few of his favorite pieces. "You'll need these for comfort," he said, handing Sammy a hoodie and a pair of soft, cozy socks. "And maybe a few emergency snacks... you never know when you'll need a cookie or two."

Sammy took the snacks with a grin, putting them carefully in his suitcase. "Thanks, Munch. I'll definitely need these for study breaks."

Snatch, who was usually more reserved, cleared his throat and held up a small, mismatched pair of socks from Sammy's drawer. "These have been some of my favourites over the years," he said, handing them to Sammy. "They've been through many adventures. Don't forget your roots, even if they're a bit... colorful."

Sammy chuckled as he added the socks to his suitcase. He remembered how Snatch would borrow socks for his "secret collection" and how he'd often find them stashed in funny places. Somehow, those socks felt like little pieces of home.

As they reminisced, Sammy found himself holding a glitter-covered notebook—the one they'd used to write down all their plans for adventures. He flipped through the pages, filled with sketches, lists, and ideas. He saw reminders of their scavenger hunts, their glitter-bomb parties, and notes on monster hide-and-seek strategies.

Whiffle's fur sparkled with excitement. "I remember that notebook! We filled it with ideas we never even got to try."

Sammy's heart swelled with warmth. "You know, maybe I'll bring this with me. I can write down new adventures we'll have together... even if they're a little different this time."

The monsters nodded, their eyes shining with appreciation. They all knew that Sammy going to college didn't mean their friendship was ending, but rather, it was changing. And change, while sometimes bittersweet, didn't have to be a goodbye.

As the packing continued, each monster took a turn reminiscing about their favorite memories. Munch reminded Sammy of the time they'd had a late-night snack feast, sneaking into the kitchen for a "secret midnight meal." Blinky recalled the time they'd put on a play in the living room, complete with costumes and props, turning their world into a magical theatre.

They laughed and joked, each memory bringing them closer together even as Sammy's departure loomed.

When they finally packed up the last of his belongings, Sammy looked around at the boxes and bags, a mixture of excitement and sadness filling his heart. He glanced at his friends, realizing just how much they'd shaped his childhood. They were his companions, his confidantes, his secret-keepers. How would he face college without them?

Sensing his emotions, Whiffle reached out and took Sammy's hand. "You'll do great, Sammy. And remember, we're always with you, even if we're not physically there."

Munch nodded, offering one of his snacks. "And when you need a snack, just think of me. I'll be there in spirit, making sure you're well-fed!"

Blinky's glow softened, a warm, gentle light that filled the room. "Every time you need guidance, remember all we've been through together. We're a part of you, Sammy."

Snatch adjusted his hat and smiled. "And you know us, we always find a way. Just because you're going to college doesn't mean we can't visit from time to time."

Sammy felt his eyes prickling with tears as he hugged each of his friends tightly, not quite ready to say goodbye but knowing he had to.

"Thank you, all of you. I wouldn't be who I am without you. And I promise, I'll keep our adventures going, no matter where I am."

As they stood together in a quiet, tearful embrace, Sammy's mom called from downstairs, signalling that it was time for dinner.

The monsters gave him one last round of hugs, each one feeling a mix of pride, love, and a touch of sadness. They watched as he took one final look around his room, his gaze lingering on the small keepsakes and mementos of their shared memories. Then, with a deep breath, Sammy headed downstairs, leaving the room filled with the warmth of his monster friends and their unbreakable bond.

As Sammy left, the monsters gathered together, making a quiet promise to each other.

"Sammy may be going to college," Whiffle said, his voice full of determination, "but that doesn't mean our adventures are over."

Blinky nodded, his glow shimmering with hope. "Wherever he goes, we'll find ways to bring him a little magic."

Snatch lifted his hat in a salute. "To Sammy's new adventures—and to us, the friends who'll always be there for him."

And with that, the monsters faded into the cozy corners of Sammy's room, each one filled with excitement, hope, and a promise to keep the magic alive, no matter how far their friend might go.

As Sammy sat down at the dinner table, he couldn't help but smile. Somewhere deep inside, he knew that this wasn't a goodbye—it was the start of a new chapter, one that would still be filled with laughter, friendship, and magic.

Chapter 2: Dorm Room Surprises

Moving into his college dorm had been both thrilling and overwhelming for Sammy. The campus buzzed with energy, with students unpacking, introducing themselves, and exploring. Sammy's dorm room was small but cozy, with two beds, two desks, and a closet squeezed in. He shared the space with his new roommate, Jake, who was friendly and easy-going. Yet, as Sammy unpacked his last box, he couldn't help but feel a pang of homesickness, thinking about his monster friends.

He'd barely settled in when he noticed something unusual: a faint trail of glitter leading from his desk to the window.

Sammy blinked, thinking maybe he was imagining things. But as he looked closer, he saw it—tiny flecks of silver and blue glitter that sparkled just like the kind Glimmerpuff used to leave. His heart leapt with excitement and disbelief.

Could it be?

He followed the glitter trail, tiptoeing across the small space. The trail led him to his windowsill, where he found what looked like a small paw print, dusted in blue sparkles. Sammy's heart raced. There was no mistaking it. Somehow, his monster friends had managed to find him at college.

Just then, Jake walked in, holding two steaming cups of coffee. "Hey, Sammy! Brought you a coffee," Jake said, smiling as he set one down on the desk. He glanced at Sammy, who was still inspecting the windowsill.

"Uh, did you find something?" Jake asked, raising an eyebrow.

Sammy quickly shook his head and forced a casual smile. "Oh, uh, no, nothing! Just... admiring the view," he said, grabbing the coffee to cover up his surprise.

Jake didn't seem to notice Sammy's flustered response. "Well, let's explore campus after we finish unpacking. Gotta figure out where everything is, right?"

Sammy nodded, his mind already racing. "Yeah, sounds great! I'll catch up in a bit."

As soon as Jake left the room, Sammy went back to the windowsill. He lightly touched the glittery paw print, smiling to himself. It was unmistakable. His friends had found him, and if he knew them well, there were probably a few more surprises waiting.

The Glitter Trail and Hidden Messages

Sammy decided to follow the glitter trail more carefully, curious to see where it would lead. As he traced the faint sparkles along the floor, he noticed that they looped around his desk and led up to one of his notebooks.

He flipped open the cover, and his eyes widened in surprise. There, in faint, glittery letters, was a message:

"We're here, Sammy! Get ready for college, monster-style! — Glimmerpuff & Friends"

Sammy grinned, a warmth spreading through him. He turned the page and found a tiny doodle of Whiffle, drawn in shimmery blue ink, holding a sign that read "Room Sweet Room!" He chuckled, knowing that Whiffle had probably been as excited as he was to see the new dorm room.

Just as he closed the notebook, he heard a quiet, familiar whisper from under the bed.

"Psst... Sammy!"

Sammy crouched down and looked under the bed, his heart pounding with excitement. He spotted a familiar pair of twinkling eyes and soft, round ears.

"Mumbles!" Sammy whispered, beaming as he reached out to his friend.

Mumbles, the whispering monster, peeked out, grinning shyly as he waved. "We couldn't let you come here alone," he whispered, his voice soft as ever. "We just had to sneak in for a little visit."

Sammy glanced around, half-expecting to see more of his friends. "Are the others here too?"

Mumbles nodded, his eyes twinkling. "Just wait... they wanted to leave you a few surprises before saying hello."

More Friendly Clues

Sammy and Mumbles quietly followed the glitter trail through the dorm room, making sure Jake was nowhere in sight. The trail led them to Sammy's bed, where he found a small piece of paper hidden under his pillow. Written in a familiar, looping script were the words:

"When you need a laugh, we'll be right here."

Sammy couldn't help but chuckle. "That has to be from Snatch," he said, smiling. Snatch had always been one for dramatic entrances, and his notes were always filled with a touch of mystery. Sammy lifted his pillow and saw something even more surprising—one of Snatch's mismatched socks, left behind as a little reminder of home.

Mumbles whispered, "Snatch wanted you to have something cozy to remember us by."

As Sammy continued exploring, he noticed another tiny footprint on his bookshelf, this time with a hint of orange glitter. He knew right away it had to be from Munch. Sure enough, when he opened his top drawer, he found a small stash of crackers and a note:

"For midnight snack emergencies. You're welcome!"

Sammy laughed softly, holding up a cracker and silently thanking Munch for his thoughtfulness. His friends had truly thought of everything.

A Glowing Surprise

Just as Sammy was marveling at the snacks, a gentle blue glow filled the room. He looked around, confused at first, then noticed that his bedside lamp was flickering softly. As he got closer, he saw Blinky, glowing faintly, nestled beside the lamp.

"Blinky!" Sammy whispered excitedly.

Blinky grinned, his glow brightening slightly. "Surprise! I wanted to make sure you always had a little light here... especially on late study nights," he whispered. "It's a charm I left on your lamp. Just think of me whenever you need a bit of extra glow."

Sammy felt his heart swell with appreciation. Blinky had always been his guide, lighting the way during every adventure. It felt right that he'd continue to do so, even in this new chapter of Sammy's life.

A Last, Fuzzy Hello

As Sammy finished exploring each little surprise, he heard a soft thud near the closet. Turning around, he spotted Whiffle, covered in a light dusting of blue glitter, giving him a sheepish wave.

"Hey, Sammy," Whiffle said softly, his voice warm and familiar. "Couldn't leave without saying hello myself. We all missed you, you know."

Sammy knelt down, giving Whiffle a tight hug. "I missed you guys too. It wouldn't be the same here without you."

Whiffle pulled back, smiling with a hint of mischief. "And don't worry, we'll still find ways to visit. We've got our own little hiding spots on campus now." He winked. "We'll be around whenever you need us."

Just then, they heard footsteps approaching—the unmistakable sound of Jake returning to the room. Sammy quickly motioned for Whiffle, Blinky, and Mumbles to hide. The monsters vanished into the shadows, leaving only faint traces of glitter in their wake.

Jake entered, carrying a box of supplies. He glanced around, frowning slightly. "Did you spill glitter or something? It's all over your side of the room."

Sammy laughed, covering up his surprise with a casual shrug. "Oh, must have been from one of my boxes. Guess some glittery stuff got mixed in."

Jake shrugged, unfazed. "Hey, no worries. Adds some sparkle, right?"

As Jake went back to unpacking, Sammy stole a glance at the faint shimmer of glitter near his desk and the gentle glow on his bedside lamp. Though his friends were hidden, he could feel their presence, filling the room with warmth and memories.

Settling In with a Little Magic

That night, as Sammy lay in bed, he took a moment to reflect on the day's discoveries. Each little surprise, each shimmer of glitter, felt like a promise—a reminder that his monster friends would be with him, no matter where he went.

He whispered softly to the room, knowing his friends were listening. "Thanks for finding me. College wouldn't be the same without you."

A soft breeze rustled the papers on his desk, and Sammy could have sworn he heard a faint, familiar whisper in response: "We're always here, Sammy."

With a smile, he drifted off to sleep, his heart full of warmth, friendship, and a hint of magic that only his monster friends could bring.

Chapter 3: The First College Scavenger Hunt

The first few days of college had been a whirlwind for Sammy. Between meeting new people, finding his way around campus, and settling into classes, he hadn't had much time to catch his breath. But one morning, as he was getting ready for the day, he found a mysterious note tucked under his pillow.

The note was written in a familiar, loopy script:

"Welcome to the First College Scavenger Hunt! Ready to explore? Follow the clues and find some familiar monster magic along the way. First clue: Check the place where books never sleep!"

Sammy's heart raced with excitement. His monster friends had put together a scavenger hunt just for him! A warm feeling of home washed over him, knowing they were still watching out for him, even here.

He grinned, pocketing the note and heading toward the campus library—where else would "books never sleep"?

Clue #1: The Campus Library

Sammy arrived at the library, marveling at its tall, sunlit windows and towering shelves. As he stepped inside, he remembered the countless adventures he'd had with his friends in his old room, huddled over books and coming up with plans for scavenger hunts and silly mysteries.

He scanned the rows of bookshelves, wondering where the clue could be hidden. Just as he rounded a corner in the fiction section, he saw a faint sparkle near one of the shelves. A small, glittery envelope was tucked between two books—A Tale of Two Cities and The Secret Garden. Sammy pulled it out, feeling a burst of excitement as he opened it.

Inside was a note in Blinky's neat handwriting:

"The journey continues! For your next clue, find the place where people gather to fuel their brains and satisfy their cravings. Hint: Snacks await!"

Sammy laughed, knowing that only Munch could have come up with that clue. He immediately knew where to go next—the campus café.

Clue #2: The Campus Café

The café was buzzing with students grabbing coffee and breakfast before their morning classes. Sammy walked in, scanning the tables and counters for any hint of glitter or sparkle. The smell of coffee and fresh pastries filled the air, and he couldn't help but feel a pang of nostalgia for all the late-night snack raids he'd had with Munch back home.

Near the condiment station, Sammy noticed a small, glittery paw print on the sugar packets. Sure enough, there was another tiny envelope, hidden under a pile of napkins.

He opened it and found a note in Munch's handwriting:

"Good job, Sammy! You found my favorite place on campus. Now, your next clue is hiding where people like to run, play, and breathe in fresh air. I'll give you a hint: Look near something tall and shady."

Sammy thought for a moment, then smiled. That had to be the old oak tree by the track and field area. He'd seen it on his first day during orientation, a huge, sprawling tree that cast a wide, shady circle on the grass.

Clue #3: The Old Oak Tree

Sammy made his way over to the track and field area, which was mostly empty this early in the morning. The oak tree stood proudly near the edge, its branches stretching out like welcoming arms. As he approached, he noticed a bit of shimmering glitter on one of the lower branches.

Hanging from a thin thread was a small, sparkling feather—a signature from Whiffle. Sammy carefully took it down, smiling as he thought of his fluffy friend who always seemed to love hiding in cozy corners.

The feather was attached to another note:

"Nice work, adventurer! Now it's time to test your wits. Find the place where knowledge flows freely, and look for something that glows."

Sammy immediately thought of the science building, where the classrooms and labs were filled with all kinds of fascinating equipment. He had a feeling that Blinky had left him something special there.

Clue #4: The Science Building

The science building was bustling with students moving between labs and classrooms. Sammy walked in, carefully looking around for any sign of Blinky's glow. He followed his intuition down a quiet hallway to the physics lab, where a soft blue glow caught his eye.

In the back corner, near a set of glass beakers, Sammy spotted another envelope with Blinky's faint glow shimmering around it. He gently picked it up, marveling at the subtle magic that only Blinky could create.

Opening the envelope, Sammy read the next clue:

"Almost there, Sammy! Your last stop is where students go to relax, laugh, and sometimes even perform. Find the stage, and you'll find your final prize!"

Sammy knew exactly where to go—the outdoor amphitheatre, where students often gathered for open mic nights and performances.

Clue #5: The Amphitheatre

The amphitheatre was a beautiful, open space surrounded by a circle of trees and benches. The stone stage looked inviting, and as Sammy approached, he saw the faintest hint of glitter scattered around the steps leading up to it.

In the center of the stage was a small, wrapped package tied with a glittery ribbon. Sammy's heart swelled with gratitude and excitement as he walked up and picked it up, carefully unwrapping it.

Inside was a small, handcrafted booklet titled "Adventures Await: College Edition." Each page was filled with sketches, notes, and little messages from his monster friends:

Whiffle's Page had a cozy little illustration of Whiffle lounging under a blanket fort, with a note that read, "Find cozy corners for studying. And don't forget to take breaks for daydreams!"

Munch's Page was decorated with tiny illustrations of snacks and read, "Keep snacks on hand for study sessions and late nights. And remember, there's always time for a snack break!"

Blinky's Page glowed faintly, with a sketch of a glowing lamp and the words, "Whenever you need guidance, remember the light we've shared. You're never truly alone."

Snatch's Page was adorned with a tiny drawing of his top hat and read, "Keep a bit of magic and mystery wherever you go. College is as much about adventure as it is about learning."

At the very end of the booklet, there was a group message written in glittery ink:

"Dear Sammy, we might not be with you physically, but we're always here, just a sparkle or glow away. College will be full of new adventures, and we'll be cheering you on every step of the way. Enjoy every moment, and know that we'll find ways to surprise you. Love, Your Monster Friends."

Sammy felt his eyes sting with tears as he read their words. The booklet was more than just a reminder of his friends—it was a promise that, no matter how far he went, they'd always find ways to support him and keep the magic alive.

As he held the booklet close, he noticed a final little note on the back cover:

"P.S. If you ever need us, just leave a little glitter trail."

A Heartfelt Thank You

Sammy sat on the amphitheatre steps, feeling a comforting presence as he thought of each of his friends and the effort they'd put into creating this scavenger hunt. It was as though they'd carefully placed bits of themselves in his new world, reminding him that while things were changing, their friendship was as strong as ever.

He whispered softly to the air, hoping they could hear him, "Thank you, Whiffle, Munch, Blinky, Snatch, and everyone. I'm so lucky to have you all in my life."

With the little booklet tucked safely in his backpack, Sammy stood up, ready to face whatever college life had in store for him. And as he walked back across campus, he couldn't help but smile, knowing that somewhere, his monster friends were watching over him, cheering him on from the shadows and corners, leaving trails of glitter and magic along the way.

Chapter 4: The Invisible Roommate

A few weeks into college, Sammy was getting used to life in his dorm room. He was enjoying his classes, exploring campus, and settling into a routine with his roommate, Jake. Jake was friendly and laid-back, making it easy for Sammy to feel at home. Still, every now and then, Sammy would notice something odd around the room—a slight rustling, a faint whisper, or the feeling of someone watching him. It wasn't unsettling exactly, just... unusual.

One evening, as Sammy was finishing up some homework, he felt a soft tap on his shoulder. He turned, but no one was there.

Then he heard a faint, familiar whisper.

"Psst... Sammy."

Sammy grinned, instantly recognizing the quiet, breathy voice. "Mumbles! Is that you?"

A soft shimmer appeared in the air, and a pair of glimmering eyes blinked at him from what seemed like thin air. Mumbles, his shy, whispering monster friend, let out a soft chuckle as he made himself slightly visible.

"Surprise!" Mumbles whispered, grinning. "I couldn't let you go to college without a little monster company."

Sammy's heart warmed with gratitude. He hadn't expected any of his friends to stick around for more than a quick visit, but Mumbles had quietly moved into his dorm. "You're really here? Mumbles, that's amazing!"

Mumbles nodded, his form shimmering faintly before fading back to invisibility. "I figured I could keep you company without anyone noticing. Besides, it's fun being an 'invisible roommate'—the kind of roommate who can help you find things, play a few pranks, and keep you smiling."

Sammy laughed, knowing Mumbles would be a perfect blend of comfort and mischief. But before he could respond, the door opened, and Jake walked in, carrying a bag of snacks.

"Hey, Sammy," Jake said, tossing a bag of chips onto his desk. "You talking to someone?"

Sammy quickly turned, hoping to cover up his surprise. "Oh! Uh, no, just, uh, talking to myself. You know, trying to memorize stuff for class."

Jake raised an eyebrow but shrugged it off. "Whatever works, man."

As soon as Jake was distracted by his phone, Sammy glanced around for Mumbles, wondering how they could keep his presence a secret. Mumbles, as if reading his mind, let out a soft giggle and whispered, "Don't worry, Sammy. I'm pretty good at hiding. I'll just... blend in."

And from that moment, Mumbles became Sammy's invisible, secret roommate, making life in college both comforting and unexpectedly hilarious.

Invisible Pranks and Secret Help

Mumbles wasted no time in creating a little fun in the dorm room. One night, while Jake was studying, Mumbles nudged Jake's coffee cup just an inch or two closer to his hand every time he looked away. Jake blinked, confused, as he noticed his cup "magically" moving toward him.

"Uh, Sammy, did you see that?" Jake asked, his face twisted in confusion.

Sammy held back a laugh. "See what?"

"My coffee... it keeps moving. Must be tired or something." Jake gave a nervous chuckle, looking around suspiciously.

From behind the chair, Sammy heard Mumbles whisper a quiet giggle, clearly enjoying his invisible antics. Sammy grinned, trying to keep his expression casual. With Mumbles around, every day seemed to hold a new surprise.

The Case of the "Vanishing" Snacks

Jake wasn't the only target of Mumbles' playful pranks. One night, while Sammy was working on a late-night paper, Mumbles decided to offer some "assistance" in the form of snack retrieval.

Sammy had placed a bag of pretzels on his desk, but every time he reached for it, the bag seemed to move an inch further out of reach. After the third attempt, he saw the faintest outline of Mumbles, carefully pushing the bag just beyond his grasp.

"Mumbles!" Sammy whispered with a grin, trying not to wake Jake. "Are you trying to help or tease?"

Mumbles chuckled, his voice soft and playful. "A little of both. You looked like you needed a stretch."

They shared a quiet laugh, and Sammy finally managed to grab his pretzels. Having Mumbles around made even simple tasks like grabbing a snack feel like a small, joyful adventure.

Invisible Antics During Room Checks

One afternoon, Jake mentioned that the Resident Advisor would be doing a surprise room check. This meant that Sammy had to find a way to keep Mumbles completely hidden and avoid any accidental pranks.

"Alright, Mumbles, we've got a room check today," Sammy whispered. "Maybe just, I don't know, stay as invisible as possible?"

Mumbles, who'd been making paper airplanes out of Sammy's spare notes, nodded enthusiastically. "Invisible, got it! I'll be like a shadow's shadow," he whispered, giggling softly.

When the RA came in to inspect the room, Mumbles did an excellent job staying hidden… except for one tiny incident. Just as the RA turned to inspect Sammy's side of the room, Mumbles accidentally nudged a loose pencil, sending it rolling across the desk.

The RA glanced at the pencil, slightly confused, but shrugged it off. "You guys are all set. Just, uh, keep things neat, okay?"

As soon as the RA left, Sammy and Mumbles let out a sigh of relief, sharing a silent laugh. Mumbles had done his best, but staying perfectly hidden wasn't always easy for an invisible monster with a love for mischief.

The Floating Scarf

One chilly morning, Jake couldn't find his scarf before heading out. He searched his side of the room, tossing clothes and books everywhere. Sammy, who knew Jake's habits well, noticed the scarf had been left on the back of the chair.

Just as he was about to point it out, Mumbles whispered, "Let me help!"

Before Sammy could respond, Jake turned around to see his scarf hovering in mid-air, as though lifted by an invisible hand. His eyes widened, and he froze.

"Uh... Sammy?" Jake's voice shook a little. "Is my scarf... floating?"

Thinking quickly, Sammy tried to keep a straight face. "Oh! I read something about static electricity making things levitate in the winter," he said, hoping to calm Jake down. "It's, uh, science. Here, let me grab it for you."

Jake nodded, looking unconvinced but taking the scarf cautiously. As he left, he glanced back once more, looking bewildered. As soon as the door shut, Sammy and Mumbles burst into silent laughter.

"Okay, maybe I shouldn't have made it float," Mumbles admitted, his voice barely a whisper as he giggled. "But his face was priceless!"

Sammy wiped away a tear of laughter. "I think you might give Jake a few ghost stories to tell."

The Secret Friend

Over the next few weeks, Mumbles continued to add little touches of magic to Sammy's life. From rearranging Sammy's notes into perfectly organized piles during study sessions, to moving his coffee mug just an inch closer when he seemed tired, Mumbles proved to be both a helpful and hilariously mischievous companion.

Whenever Sammy was feeling homesick or overwhelmed, Mumbles would appear by his side, his quiet whispers and comforting presence a reminder of all the adventures they'd shared together. In a strange way, Mumbles made the dorm room feel more like home.

One evening, as they were winding down, Sammy spoke softly to Mumbles. "Thanks for sticking around, Mumbles. College is exciting, but it's nice to have a piece of home here with me."

Mumbles gave a quiet, heartfelt hum, his voice as soft as a lullaby. "You're welcome, Sammy. I'll always be here to bring a little magic… and maybe a little mischief too."

Just as he said that, Mumbles playfully nudged Sammy's pen, making it roll off the desk. Sammy laughed, catching it in mid-air.

"I wouldn't expect anything less," Sammy whispered, a big grin spreading across his face.

As he got into bed, Sammy felt a warm sense of comfort. His invisible roommate had made college life unexpectedly magical, full of laughter, pranks, and quiet companionship. And as he drifted off to sleep, he knew that with Mumbles by his side, he'd never truly be alone.

With a bit of sparkle, a lot of whispers, and the comfort of an old friend, Sammy's college experience was turning out to be everything he'd hoped for—and so much more.

Chapter 5: The Late-Night Library Mystery

It was a chilly Friday night, and Sammy had planned to spend a quiet evening in his dorm room. But as he was settling in with his books, Mumbles, his invisible monster friend, whispered, "Psst... Sammy, ever heard of the secret room in the library?"

Sammy looked up, intrigued. "A secret room? I've been to the library a dozen times and never seen anything like that."

Mumbles grinned, his eyes sparkling with excitement. "Well, it's not exactly on the library map, but I heard it's hidden somewhere in the basement. They say it's filled with old, mysterious books that no one's read in centuries. Rumour has it, there's even a portal to other realms."

Sammy's heart raced with excitement. A hidden room full of mysteries and secrets? He couldn't resist. "Mumbles, this sounds amazing! Let's go check it out."

As they snuck out of the dorm and made their way across campus, Sammy felt a familiar glow beside him. Blinky had joined them, his soft blue light illuminating the path.

"You'll need me for this one," Blinky said, winking. "A place like that is bound to be dark, and who knows what kinds of secrets are hidden there?"

Together, Sammy, Mumbles, and Blinky set off on their late-night adventure, heading straight for the library.

Into the Library's Shadows

The library was quiet at this hour, the soft hum of fluorescent lights and the faint smell of old books filling the air. They made their way past the main shelves and down a narrow staircase that led to the basement, where rows of untouched, dusty books lined the walls.

Blinky's glow cast gentle shadows as they walked, giving the basement an eerie but enchanting feel. Mumbles moved silently beside them, his whispers barely audible. "They say only a few students have ever found the room, and none of them are sure how they did it. It's hidden behind a bookshelf, they think."

"Perfect," Sammy whispered back, his heart pounding. "Let's start looking!"

They scanned each row carefully, peering behind every dusty shelf and checking every corner. After a few minutes, Blinky noticed something odd: a single shelf that didn't seem as dusty as the others. The books on this shelf looked ancient but well-preserved, as though someone had touched them recently.

Blinky floated closer, his glow illuminating the spines. "I think we're onto something," he murmured.

Sammy carefully pulled out an old, leather-bound book with faded gold lettering. As he did, he heard a soft click. Suddenly, the shelf shifted, revealing a narrow doorway behind it.

They exchanged excited glances, then slipped through the opening, entering the hidden room.

The Secret Room of Mysteries

The room was like stepping into another world. Walls lined with ancient books, scrolls, and strange artifacts greeted them. The air was thick with the smell of parchment and ink, and soft candlelight flickered on the walls, giving the room a warm but mysterious glow.

Blinky's light grew brighter, revealing a massive, worn-out table in the center of the room. A large, open book lay on the table, with symbols and diagrams they couldn't quite understand.

Sammy ran his fingers over the book's pages, marveling at the intricate illustrations of creatures, plants, and stars. "This... this must be a book of ancient knowledge," he whispered, awestruck.

Mumbles floated close, whispering, "Look at this!" He pointed to a dusty scroll tied with a ribbon, tucked beside the book.

Sammy carefully picked it up and untied the ribbon, unfurling the scroll. The paper was delicate, covered in beautiful, swirling handwriting that read:

"To those who seek the secrets of the universe, let light guide your way. Seek the Guardian's Key and the Stars' Path will reveal itself."

"The Guardian's Key?" Sammy wondered aloud. "What could that be?"

Blinky moved closer to a nearby shelf, where he spotted a strange, glimmering key in the shape of a star. He floated over, nudging it with his glow. "I think this might be it."

Sammy took the key, feeling a warmth radiate from it. The key was beautifully crafted, with tiny gemstones embedded along the edges, sparkling in Blinky's light. It felt almost alive in his hands.

The Mysterious Portal

As Sammy held the key, he noticed a small, engraved panel on the wall, shaped like a star. He looked at Blinky and Mumbles, who both nodded in encouragement.

He carefully placed the key into the panel, and with a soft hum, the room began to shift. The wall in front of them shimmered and faded, revealing what looked like a doorway into another realm. Stars sparkled around the edges of the portal, and faint, distant music filled the air.

"Whoa…" Sammy breathed, captivated by the sight. The portal seemed to open onto a shimmering forest, where glowing creatures moved among towering trees.

Mumbles' voice was barely a whisper. "The legends are true. The portal leads to a magical realm."

But as they stepped closer, the shimmering light began to dim, and the portal seemed to fade slightly. It was as if the doorway was losing power, its connection weakening.

Blinky, noticing the dimming glow, leaned in. "I think it only opens fully when certain conditions are met. Maybe there's a way to strengthen the light?"

Sammy looked around, then spotted a small, ancient-looking lantern on the table, covered in runes. "This must be it. Maybe it powers the portal?"

He carefully lit the lantern, and as it started to glow, the portal flared back to life, the stars along the edges sparkling even brighter.

With one last glance at his friends, Sammy took a deep breath and stepped forward. But just as he reached the edge of the portal, they heard footsteps echoing in the library above.

"Uh-oh!" Mumbles whispered, his eyes wide. "Someone's coming!"

A Close Call

Reluctantly, Sammy stepped back from the portal. He wanted nothing more than to explore the other realm, but the footsteps were getting louder. They had to leave.

"Quick, put everything back!" Sammy whispered.

Blinky doused the lantern, and the portal faded from sight, leaving only the faint outline of the doorway. Sammy returned the key to the shelf, and Mumbles helped straighten the old scroll and book. In just a few seconds, the room looked as untouched as they had found it.

They slipped out of the secret room, closing the hidden door behind them just as the librarian entered the basement. She glanced at them suspiciously but didn't say a word as they made their way back up the stairs.

Once they were safely outside, they stopped to catch their breath, still buzzing with excitement from what they'd discovered.

Secrets for Another Day

As they walked back to the dorm, Sammy couldn't stop thinking about the hidden room, the Guardian's Key, and the portal to the other realm. It was a world filled with secrets, and he was certain he'd barely scratched the surface.

Blinky floated beside him, his glow soft but filled with excitement. "Do you think we'll go back?" he asked, his voice full of wonder.

Sammy nodded, grinning. "Definitely. That room is too amazing to leave unexplored. I think it's got secrets waiting just for us."

Mumbles smiled, his whisper filled with excitement. "Next time, we'll figure out how to open the portal completely. Who knows what's waiting on the other side?"

They reached the dorm just as the sky began to lighten, their minds buzzing with plans for future adventures. Sammy knew that, with his friends by his side, college life was bound to hold just as much magic and mystery as all their past adventures. And that secret room in the library? It was only the beginning.

As they parted ways to rest, Sammy thought about the note they'd found in the secret room: "Seek the Guardian's Key and the Stars' Path will reveal itself."

He didn't know what it all meant yet, but he was more than ready to find out.

Chapter 6: The Haunted Study Session

Midterms were approaching, and Sammy had his first real college test looming. His desk was piled high with textbooks, lecture notes, and a seemingly endless list of topics to review. He felt a mixture of stress and exhaustion as he tried to memorize equations and definitions, his head buzzing with information overload.

Sighing, he rubbed his eyes and leaned back in his chair. "If only studying could be... a little more exciting," he mumbled to himself.

As if on cue, a soft, familiar whisper drifted through the room. "Need a little help, Sammy?"

Sammy grinned, looking up to see a faint shimmer in the air. Mumbles, Blinky, Whiffle, and even Munch had gathered around, each of them glowing with mischievous excitement.

"Haunting your study session could be just the thing you need," Mumbles whispered with a playful twinkle in his eyes.

Blinky, glowing with enthusiasm, nodded. "Studying doesn't have to be boring! We'll make sure it's a night to remember."

Sammy laughed, feeling a surge of warmth. "Alright, you little study ghosts. Let's do it! Just don't scare me too much—I actually need to learn this stuff!"

The monsters exchanged grins, each of them eager to add their own magical touch to Sammy's late-night study session.

The Haunted Textbook Pages

Whiffle started things off, picking up one of Sammy's heavy textbooks and flipping it open to the chapter on history. With a soft hum, he concentrated, and suddenly the words on the page began to shift and shimmer, forming tiny moving pictures.

Sammy's eyes widened in delight as he watched scenes from history unfold right on the page. Miniature soldiers marched across a battlefield, kings and queens waved from tiny thrones, and famous monuments seemed to rise out of the text.

"Whoa, Whiffle! This is amazing!" Sammy whispered, watching as the tiny figures moved across the page. Each scene brought the history lesson to life, making it feel more like a story than a study session.

Whiffle beamed. "Just a little magic to make history memorable!"

As Sammy took notes, the illustrations helped him visualize key events, and he found himself remembering more details than he ever had before.

The Mysterious Math Problems

Next, Munch decided to help with Sammy's math notes. Sammy had been struggling to memorize equations all night, and Munch's solution was to make things a little more... active.

With a mischievous grin, Munch tapped his paws on Sammy's notebook, and suddenly the numbers began to float up off the page, rearranging themselves in mid-air. Equations hovered around Sammy, dancing and twirling like they were performing a magical math ballet.

Sammy chuckled, watching as numbers floated past him, rearranging themselves into different problems. "Munch, you're a genius! This actually makes math fun."

Munch puffed up proudly, snacking on a cookie he'd somehow managed to sneak in. "Numbers can be tasty too!" he said with a wink, tossing Sammy a bite-sized snack for encouragement.

Sammy worked through the floating equations, enjoying the challenge of catching numbers and fitting them into place. By the end of it, he was surprised at how much he'd learned.

Spelling Specters and Vocabulary Ghosts

Mumbles took over the English section of Sammy's notes, helping him with vocabulary and literary terms. He whispered softly, his voice wrapping around Sammy's vocabulary list like a gentle breeze.

"Each word has its own spirit, Sammy," Mumbles said with a smile. "Listen closely, and they'll speak to you."

As Sammy looked at the list, each word glowed faintly and whispered its own meaning in a ghostly voice. Words like "effervescent," "quixotic," and "ethereal" floated in the air, whispering their definitions in soft, echoing tones. Sammy found himself captivated by each word, the haunting sounds making the vocabulary easier to remember.

By the time he'd gone through the list, he had memorized each word and its meaning as if they were old friends whispering secrets.

"Thanks, Mumbles," Sammy said, feeling both comforted and a little spooked. "You definitely know how to make words come to life."

Mumbles chuckled, fading back into the shadows. "Just a little friendly haunting," he whispered.

Glow-in-the-Dark Science Diagrams

Blinky was eager to help with Sammy's science notes. With a mischievous twinkle in his eye, he hovered over Sammy's biology textbook, which was open to the chapter on cell structure.

"Let me light things up for you," Blinky said with a grin, concentrating as his glow intensified.

With a flicker, Blinky's glow cast shimmering, glow-in-the-dark illustrations onto the wall. Cell structures, the layers of the atmosphere, and even the solar system appeared in brilliant colors, each one glowing with detail. The diagrams moved and shifted as Blinky's glow flowed around the room, making the science concepts come alive.

Sammy watched in awe, fascinated by the glowing visuals. He could see each part of a cell as if it were right in front of him—the nucleus, mitochondria, and even the tiny ribosomes moving like they were part of a cosmic dance.

"This makes everything so clear, Blinky!" Sammy said, furiously jotting down notes. "I wish you could come to all my science classes."

Blinky laughed, casting a gentle glow over Sammy's notebook. "Anytime you need a little light, you know where to find me."

A Goodnight Ghostly Review

As the clock ticked past midnight, Sammy leaned back, feeling a strange mixture of exhaustion and joy. His monster friends had made the study session magical, helping him absorb more information than he thought possible.

But they had one final surprise up their sleeves.

Just as Sammy was closing his textbook, a gentle hum filled the air, and each monster appeared around him, shimmering with soft, colorful light. Together, they started a quiet "review chant," each taking turns to repeat the key points from each subject.

Whiffle recited a brief summary of the history timeline, Munch whispered important equations, Mumbles softly repeated vocabulary definitions, and Blinky illuminated the cell structures one last time.

Sammy closed his eyes, letting the words and images wash over him, feeling as if they were imprinting themselves in his mind. It was like a magical lullaby of knowledge, each concept settling in his memory with ease.

When they finished, Sammy opened his eyes and smiled at his friends. "You guys are incredible. I think I might actually be ready for this test."

Mumbles patted him on the shoulder, whispering, "We believe in you, Sammy. And if you ever need us, we'll be right here—haunting your notes whenever you need a boost."

With a yawn, Sammy thanked each of them, feeling a deep sense of gratitude. His friends had made a daunting night of studying feel fun and magical, reminding him that even the most challenging moments could be filled with laughter and warmth.

A Magical Memory to Last

As he drifted off to sleep that night, Sammy's dreams were filled with dancing equations, glowing science diagrams, and words whispering their meanings. It was as if the night's magic had seeped into his mind, each memory shining brightly in his dreams.

When he woke up the next morning, he felt surprisingly refreshed and confident. Sammy knew his friends had given him more than just help with studying—they'd left him with memories that would stay with him forever.

With a smile, he gathered his notes and headed to class, feeling ready to tackle his midterm. No matter what happened, he knew he'd always have a little magic—and a few friendly "study ghosts"—on his side.

And as he left the dorm, he couldn't help but feel that, thanks to his monster friends, the mysteries of college life had just become a little less intimidating and a lot more enchanting.

Chapter 7: Midnight Snack Adventures

It was well past midnight, and Sammy lay in bed, wide awake. Despite the late hour, his stomach growled insistently, demanding a snack. He glanced over at Jake, his roommate, who was snoring softly, blissfully unaware of Sammy's hunger pangs. Sammy's mind drifted to the cafeteria, imagining rows of muffins, cookies, and maybe even a leftover slice of pie.

Just as he was about to give up on his midnight craving, he heard a familiar crunch from under his bed. He peered over the side and saw a small pile of crumbs—and Munch, nibbling on a cookie with a mischievous grin.

"Munch!" Sammy whispered excitedly. "Are you snacking down there?"

Munch looked up, his face lighting up with a wide smile. "Hey, Sammy! Couldn't sleep, so I thought I'd grab a little snack." He held out a cookie. "Want a bite?"

Sammy's stomach growled again, louder this time, and he laughed softly. "Actually, yes. But I was thinking something bigger. Like... a cafeteria adventure."

Munch's eyes sparkled with excitement. "A cafeteria raid? Sammy, you're speaking my language!"

Sammy slipped quietly out of bed, and the two tiptoed to the door. With Jake still sound asleep, they snuck out of the dorm, giggling like two kids with a shared secret. The campus was silent and still, the moonlight casting long shadows across the grounds as they made their way toward the cafeteria.

When they reached the building, Sammy hesitated, peering around to make sure no staff members were patrolling. "Are you sure about this, Munch?" he whispered, glancing around nervously.

Munch grinned, giving Sammy a reassuring thumbs-up. "Trust me, I've done this a thousand times. Stick with me, and we'll be snacking in no time."

With that, Munch led Sammy to a small side door. To Sammy's surprise, it was slightly ajar, as if it had been left open just for them. Munch pushed the door open and gestured for Sammy to follow.

The cafeteria was dark and quiet, rows of tables stretching into the shadows. Munch tiptoed confidently ahead, clearly in his element as he led Sammy through the familiar terrain. They snuck past the counter, heading toward the kitchen where the best snacks were hidden.

Munch spotted a row of metal cabinets and whispered, "That's where they keep the good stuff."

He tugged on one of the cabinet handles, and the door creaked open to reveal a treasure trove of snacks—granola bars, chips, cookies, and even a few candy bars. Munch's eyes sparkled with excitement as he handed Sammy a bag of chips.

"Start with these," he said with a wink. "But there's more. Much more."

They filled their hands with snacks, trying not to laugh as they stuffed their pockets and grabbed a few extra treats. Just as they were about to explore further, they heard the sound of footsteps echoing through the cafeteria.

Sammy's heart raced. He grabbed Munch, pulling him behind a counter as the footsteps grew closer. They crouched down, holding their breath, as a campus security guard entered the cafeteria, scanning the room with a flashlight.

Munch, unfazed, munched quietly on a cookie while Sammy tried to keep still, heart pounding in his chest. The guard's footsteps echoed closer, and Sammy wondered if their adventure would be cut short. But just as the guard's flashlight swept over the counter, Munch grabbed Sammy's arm and motioned for him to follow.

The guard moved on, and they slipped around the counter, heading toward the walk-in freezer. Munch's excitement was contagious, and Sammy couldn't help but grin as they snuck inside, closing the door behind them. The cold air hit them instantly, but the shelves of frozen goodies made it worth it.

Munch pointed to a stack of ice cream sandwiches. "Cold, but worth it!" he whispered, handing one to Sammy.

Sammy took the ice cream sandwich, the cold treat feeling like a reward for their stealthy efforts. He unwrapped it, savouring the sweet, creamy taste, while Munch pulled out a small pint of chocolate ice cream for himself.

They leaned against the shelves, enjoying their snacks in the chilly silence, the thrill of sneaking into the cafeteria making the moment all the sweeter. Sammy couldn't remember the last time he'd felt this adventurous, and with Munch by his side, every bite felt like part of a mischievous midnight feast.

But just as they were finishing their ice cream, they heard a loud clanging noise. Sammy looked over, eyes wide, as the freezer door creaked open slightly. The guard had returned, and his flashlight beam was now sweeping over the shelves just outside the freezer.

Munch, thinking quickly, ducked behind a stack of frozen boxes, motioning for Sammy to follow. They crouched together, doing their best to stay hidden, as the guard's shadow moved closer.

"Got any ideas?" Sammy whispered nervously.

Munch grinned, pulling a bag of frozen peas from the shelf. "Always." He held up the bag like it was a precious treasure and tossed it across the room.

The bag hit the floor with a soft thud, the noise drawing the guard's attention. As he turned to investigate, Munch grabbed Sammy's hand, and they slipped out of the freezer, darting behind the counter once more.

With the guard distracted, they quickly made their way back to the side door. They held back a laugh as they crept through the cafeteria, each step bringing them closer to freedom. Finally, they slipped out the door and back into the cool night air, both of them grinning from ear to ear.

Once they were a safe distance from the cafeteria, Sammy let out a relieved laugh. "Munch, that was incredible! I thought we'd be caught for sure."

Munch chuckled, popping another cookie into his mouth. "Please, Sammy, I know every trick in the snack heist book. That guard never stood a chance."

They sat down on a nearby bench, emptying their pockets of snacks and sharing their loot. Under the stars, they enjoyed their midnight feast, laughing over their close calls and whispering about the best treats they'd snagged.

As they munched on chips and cookies, Sammy realized that moments like these were what made college feel magical. Late-night adventures, laughter with friends, and a shared sense of mischief—these were memories he'd hold onto forever.

"Thanks, Munch," Sammy said, taking a final bite of his ice cream sandwich. "For the snacks and the adventure. I couldn't have done it without you."

Munch grinned, patting Sammy on the back. "Anytime, Sammy. As long as there are snacks to be found, I'll be there to help you find them."

With full stomachs and happy hearts, they made their way back to the dorm, quietly sneaking back into the room without waking Jake. Sammy climbed into bed, feeling both satisfied and exhilarated from their midnight escapade.

As he drifted off to sleep, he knew that, thanks to Munch, his college nights would always have a little extra flavour and a whole lot of adventure. And with that thought, Sammy fell into a peaceful, snack-fuelled slumber, already looking forward to their next late-night quest.

Chapter 8: The Campus Art Heist (Sort of)

It started as a quiet evening in Sammy's dorm room, with the soft glow of Blinky lighting up his desk while he studied. As he read, Whiffle sat nearby, observing the blank walls and plain decor of the dorm with a thoughtful expression.

After a while, Whiffle broke the silence. "Sammy, don't you think this room could use a little more... pizzazz?"

Sammy looked up, amused. "Pizzazz? What did you have in mind?"

Whiffle's eyes sparkled with excitement. "Art! Imagine some colorful paintings or a sculpture or two. It would make this place feel more like home."

Sammy chuckled, knowing exactly where this was going. "And where are we going to get art in the middle of campus?"

Whiffle's grin widened. "Well... I might have noticed some paintings in the student lounge. Just sitting there, all lonely and underappreciated. What if we, you know... borrowed one or two?"

Sammy raised an eyebrow. "Are you suggesting we pull a campus art heist?"

"Not a heist, exactly," Whiffle said, trying to sound innocent. "More like... an art rescue mission. We'll bring the pieces back, of course. Just enough time to brighten up this room a bit!"

Sammy shook his head, laughing. He knew he shouldn't encourage Whiffle's antics, but the idea of transforming his bland dorm room was too tempting to resist. "Alright, Whiffle. Let's do it. But we have to be sneaky."

Whiffle's eyes sparkled with excitement. "Leave it to me! I've got a few tricks up my sleeve."

Under the cover of darkness, Sammy and Whiffle set off toward the student lounge. They tiptoed across campus, avoiding any wandering security staff and trying to stifle their giggles. Whiffle carried a small pouch filled with glitter, "just in case," while Sammy brought along an old blanket to cover any art pieces they decided to "borrow."

The student lounge was empty, dimly lit by the glow of exit signs. Whiffle spotted their target right away—a vibrant, abstract painting hanging on the wall, full of swirling colors and shapes that looked like they'd been made just for his artistic sensibilities.

"That one!" Whiffle whispered, pointing excitedly. "It's perfect!"

Sammy sized it up, impressed by Whiffle's choice. "It does have a lot of color. Alright, let's get it down carefully."

Whiffle floated up, giving the painting a gentle nudge to see if it was loose. With a bit of effort, they managed to lift it off the wall and wrap it in the blanket Sammy had brought. Just as they were about to head back, Whiffle's gaze shifted to a nearby sculpture—a small, glitter-covered figure of a cat. His eyes widened with admiration.

"Sammy, we can't leave without the cat. It's practically begging to join us!" he whispered, already reaching for it.

Sammy chuckled, trying to be the voice of reason. "Whiffle, the painting is more than enough. We're already pushing our luck."

But Whiffle's heart was set, and before Sammy could protest, the glittery cat was tucked under his arm. "Just think of it as extra pizzazz," Whiffle said with a grin. Sammy sighed, knowing there was no talking him out of it.

They managed to sneak the painting and the sculpture back to Sammy's dorm room without being spotted. Once inside, Whiffle arranged the painting above Sammy's bed and placed the glittery cat sculpture on his desk, stepping back to admire their handiwork.

"Look at that!" Whiffle said proudly, his eyes shining. "This room has real personality now!"

Sammy had to admit, the art did make the space feel warmer and more interesting. "You're right, Whiffle. It looks amazing," he said, impressed by how the painting's colors brightened up the room.

But their joy was short-lived.

The next morning, Sammy woke to a text from his Resident Advisor (RA): "Hi, Sammy. There's been an unusual report. Some art has gone missing from the student lounge. Let me know if you hear anything."

Sammy's heart skipped a beat. He looked over at Whiffle, who was innocently admiring the painting. "Uh, Whiffle? We've got a little problem."

Whiffle blinked, puzzled. "Problem? What kind of problem?"

"They noticed the art is missing," Sammy said, showing him the text. "I don't want to get in trouble for 'borrowing' art that doesn't belong to us."

Whiffle's expression turned serious, and he nodded. "We'll have to return it. But... we can do it with style."

Sammy tilted his head, intrigued. "Style? What are you thinking?"

Whiffle grinned, pulling out his glitter pouch. "Let's make it look like the art went on its own adventure."

That night, under cover of darkness once again, they carefully wrapped up the painting and the glittery cat sculpture. Whiffle sprinkled a trail of glitter leading from the student lounge to Sammy's dorm, as if the art had decided to go for a midnight stroll on its own.

They returned the art to its rightful places, leaving behind a little extra sparkle as a calling card. Whiffle even left a note by the painting that read: "Thanks for the adventure! I'm back now, but maybe I'll go exploring again someday."

Once everything was back in place, they stood back and admired their work, stifling laughter as they imagined the puzzled reactions people would have in the morning.

The next day, the campus was buzzing with talk about the "wandering art." Students speculated that it was an elaborate prank, while others suggested that the art had a life of its own. Sammy tried to act surprised as he listened to the rumours, grateful that Whiffle's sneaky plan had worked without getting them into trouble.

Later that evening, as they relaxed in the dorm room, Sammy turned to Whiffle with a grin. "You know, I have to hand it to you—that was a pretty clever way to cover our tracks."

Whiffle beamed with pride, throwing a bit of glitter in the air for emphasis. "I told you, Sammy! A little bit of style and glitter goes a long way."

The room might not have kept its "borrowed" artwork, but the memory of their little art heist would brighten up the space for a long time. And, as Sammy drifted off to sleep that night, he couldn't help but smile, knowing that every day with Whiffle was guaranteed to be filled with a little extra magic and just the right amount of mischief.

Chapter 9: Invisible Ink Pranks 2.0

It all started when Mumbles showed up in Sammy's dorm room with a small bottle of shimmering liquid and a sly grin. The bottle was labelled "Invisible Ink—For Secret Messages and Mischief." Sammy's eyes lit up as he picked it up, shaking it slightly and watching the liquid swirl.

"Invisible ink?" Sammy asked, curious. "What's the plan, Mumbles?"

Mumbles leaned in close, his whisper barely audible. "I thought we could start a little... secret club," he said with a wink. "Just for a few close friends. We'll leave hidden messages around campus that only our club members can find."

Sammy loved the idea instantly. A secret club sounded like the perfect blend of adventure and mystery, and with invisible ink, they could leave messages for each other that no one else could see.

"We'll need to teach a few friends how to reveal the ink," Mumbles added, "but once they know, we'll be able to share clues, jokes, and even little surprises."

Sammy nodded, grinning. "Alright, let's do it! The Secret Club of Invisible Messages has officially begun."

That evening, Mumbles gave Sammy a quick lesson on using the invisible ink. They wrote a test message on a scrap of paper, then held a small blacklight over it. The message glowed faintly under the light, revealing the words "Welcome to the Secret Club."

The effect was mesmerizing, and Sammy couldn't wait to start leaving secret notes around campus. He and Mumbles decided to begin with a few close friends who shared their sense of mischief and love for surprises.

Recruiting the First Members

The next day, Sammy casually approached his friends Emma and Liam, both of whom had been in a few of his classes and were known for their fun-loving spirits.

"Hey, Emma, Liam," he said with a grin. "I've got something cool to show you. Think of it as... an invitation."

They exchanged curious glances, leaning in as Sammy handed them a slip of paper. To the naked eye, it looked blank, but when he pulled out a small blacklight and shined it over the paper, the message "Do you want to join the Secret Club?" appeared in faint, glowing letters.

Emma's eyes widened with excitement. "Are you serious? This is amazing! A secret club?"

Liam laughed, already on board. "I'm in. How does it work?"

Sammy explained that they would leave messages around campus, using invisible ink to communicate and share clues. Each member of the club would get a small blacklight keychain to reveal the hidden messages.

With their new members officially inducted, the Secret Club was underway.

The First Clues

Their first official club activity was to leave a trail of invisible clues around campus. Mumbles suggested starting with simple messages and riddles to give the members a taste of the mystery that lay ahead.

The clues started on a bench outside the library, where Sammy wrote, "To find the next clue, visit the place where knowledge grows, and look beneath the stacks."

Emma, Liam, and Sammy met up later that day to check the library bench, using their blacklight keychains to reveal the message. Excited by their discovery, they made their way to the library and checked under the shelves in the science section, where Sammy had left the next clue: "Seek the place where voices gather, and you'll find your next secret."

The trio followed each message eagerly, moving from the student lounge to the campus café and finally to a quiet corner near the art building. Each clue made them laugh, guess, and work together to solve the riddles, bringing a sense of adventure to their usual campus routines.

As they reached the final location, they found the last message waiting for them: "Congratulations, Secret Club Member! You've unlocked Level 1. Stay tuned for more."

Emma grinned, clearly thrilled. "This is the best club ever. We need more levels and more clues!"

Sammy laughed, already planning the next set of challenges with Mumbles.

Invisible Ink Pranks and Surprises

With the Secret Club officially launched, Sammy and Mumbles decided to add some playful pranks to the mix. They left invisible ink messages on class notes, doodled funny faces in the margins of textbooks, and even left surprise "good luck" notes in the pages of the library books they knew their friends would use.

One day, they even managed to leave an invisible ink message on Liam's coffee cup in the campus café. When he turned on his blacklight, the words "This coffee is enchanted! Drink up and ace your test!" appeared. Liam laughed so hard he nearly spilled his drink.

Emma, on the other hand, found a secret message on the desk in the art room. When she revealed it with her blacklight, the message read, "Your creativity is magical. Keep shining!" She smiled, touched by the encouragement, and later thanked Sammy for the boost.

The messages became a highlight of each day, bringing laughter, encouragement, and a shared sense of mystery to their campus life.

The Mysterious New Member

One evening, Sammy received a strange message written in invisible ink on his dorm room door. He hadn't left it himself, and neither had Mumbles.

The message read, "Welcome, Secret Club! You're not the only ones with tricks up your sleeves."

Sammy felt a thrill of excitement. Could someone else have discovered their club? Was there another "prankster" on campus?

When he shared the message with Emma and Liam, they were equally intrigued. "Maybe we have a rival club," Liam joked, "or maybe it's someone who wants to join."

Sammy grinned, already planning their next move. "Whoever it is, they've got some serious invisible ink skills. We'll have to step up our game."

Mumbles was delighted by the mysterious message and suggested they create a more challenging set of clues, leaving an invitation for the unknown "mystery member" to reveal themselves.

An Invitation to Mystery

The next day, Sammy and Mumbles prepared their most complex set of invisible clues yet, taking their friends on a scavenger hunt across campus. The trail led from the library to the art building, then to the science lab, with each location holding a new, hidden message.

At the final spot, they left an invitation in invisible ink: "To our mystery friend—show yourself if you wish to join us. Signed, The Secret Club."

That night, Sammy returned to his dorm to find a new message on his door, glowing faintly under his blacklight: "Challenge accepted. See you soon, Secret Club."

Sammy and Mumbles exchanged excited glances, knowing that the Secret Club had just gotten a whole lot more interesting.

From that night on, the Secret Club continued to flourish, with more hidden messages, clever pranks, and mysterious surprises popping up around campus. Sammy, Mumbles, Emma, and Liam spent their days searching for clues, solving riddles, and laughing over the latest invisible ink adventure.

As the campus buzzed with excitement over the "mysterious messages," Sammy felt a deep sense of joy, knowing that his friends, both monster and human, were by his side. The Secret Club had transformed his college experience, making each day a new, thrilling mystery.

And as he drifted off to sleep that night, he couldn't help but wonder what other invisible surprises awaited them, just waiting to be uncovered in the glow of their blacklights.

Chapter 10: Blinky the Lecture Note-Taker

It was a few weeks into the semester, and Sammy was starting to feel the pressure of college life. Between classes, assignments, and social activities, keeping up with his lecture notes had become a real challenge. He'd scribble notes as quickly as he could, but sometimes they were incomplete, and reviewing them felt overwhelming.

One evening, as he stared at his messy notes on cellular biology, Blinky floated over, his soft blue glow illuminating the pages. He studied the notes, tilting his head thoughtfully.

"You know, Sammy," Blinky said, his voice gentle, "I might be able to help with this."

Sammy looked up, grateful. "Really? How?"

Blinky gave a sly grin. "I've been practicing my glow skills. I think I could bring some of these concepts to life. Imagine if you could see them right in front of you."

Sammy's eyes widened in excitement. "Are you saying you could... project my notes?"

"Something like that," Blinky said with a wink. "Let's give it a try!"

The First Projection: Cell Structure

They started with cellular biology, one of the trickiest topics in Sammy's current course load. Blinky hovered over the notes, focusing his glow until a faint image of a cell began to appear in the air. Sammy watched, fascinated, as Blinky's glow outlined each part of the cell—the nucleus, mitochondria, and cell membrane—like a floating, holographic diagram.

"Whoa, Blinky! This is incredible," Sammy said, reaching out to trace the glowing image with his finger. "It's like I'm seeing it right in front of me."

Blinky beamed with pride. "And watch this!" With a little more concentration, he made each cell part pulse gently as he explained its function. The nucleus glowed brighter, the mitochondria began to sparkle, and the cell membrane shimmered softly.

Sammy couldn't help but smile. Seeing the cell in three-dimensional light made it easier to understand. "This is so much better than just reading my notes," he said, quickly jotting down what he was learning. "You're a genius, Blinky!"

Blinky chuckled, his glow dimming slightly in modesty. "Just a little bit of magic, that's all."

Studying in a New Light

After the success with the cell structure, Sammy and Blinky moved on to other topics. Blinky's glow grew more sophisticated with each study session, transforming Sammy's notes into animated, floating visuals.

In chemistry, Blinky helped Sammy visualize atoms, with electrons spinning around a nucleus like tiny stars in orbit. Sammy watched in awe as Blinky's light made chemical reactions unfold before his eyes, with bonds forming and breaking in shimmering, colorful displays.

Physics was next, and Blinky's glow traced the paths of projectiles and pendulums in the air, showing how energy and momentum worked together. Sammy felt like he was standing in the middle of a live science demonstration, with each new concept coming to life in vivid, glowing detail.

As he watched these glowing visuals, Sammy found himself understanding the material in ways he hadn't before. Concepts that had once seemed abstract or confusing suddenly made perfect sense when he could actually see them.

Visual Mnemonics and Memory Boosts

Blinky took his skills even further by creating visual mnemonics to help Sammy remember tricky details. For anatomy class, he projected a glowing skeleton, highlighting the bones in a different color as Sammy recited their names.

When they studied historical events, Blinky projected timelines in mid-air, each event marked with a glowing symbol—a crown for royal events, a sword for battles, and a scroll for important documents. Sammy's eyes sparkled with excitement, finding himself drawn into each subject in a way he hadn't expected.

"History is actually fun this way," Sammy said one evening, watching as Blinky's glow traced out a map of ancient civilizations. "I can see the entire timeline right in front of me."

Blinky smiled, happy to be helping. "The more you can visualize, the more you'll remember. Just think of these as glowing memory anchors!"

And it worked. When Sammy took practice quizzes or worked through assignments, he could close his eyes and recall the images, each glowing memory helping him piece together the information.

Lecture Hall Magic

One day, Sammy had an idea. "Blinky, what if you came to one of my lectures with me?"

Blinky looked intrigued. "Are you sure? I thought I might... stand out."

Sammy chuckled. "I'll keep you hidden in my backpack. But if you peek out just enough, you could help me visualize things right there in class. Think of it as... live note-taking!"

Blinky was thrilled by the idea, and the next day, he tucked himself into Sammy's backpack and went along to his biology lecture. Sammy kept the zipper slightly open, just enough for Blinky's glow to shine through without drawing attention.

As the professor talked about the process of photosynthesis, Blinky cast tiny green light waves through the zipper, forming a floating, glowing diagram of chloroplasts, with sunlight entering the cell and energy being converted. Sammy watched, captivated, as Blinky made each step of the process appear in vivid detail.

Whenever the professor introduced a new concept, Blinky projected it subtly, just enough for Sammy to see. Sammy took notes faster and more accurately, keeping up with the lecture like never before.

When the class ended, Sammy whispered to his backpack, "You were amazing, Blinky! I feel like I actually understood everything today."

Blinky chuckled softly. "Glad to be of service, Sammy. It's kind of fun, being a secret study aid!"

Creative Studying Techniques

With Blinky's help, Sammy's study methods transformed entirely. Instead of reading static notes, he now spent his study sessions with a personal light show, each concept unfolding in front of him. Blinky taught him to break down complex ideas into visual components, creating mental "scenes" for each topic.

One evening, as they reviewed Sammy's notes on the human circulatory system, Blinky created a glowing diagram of a heart, complete with pulsing lights to show the flow of blood. Watching the blood "travel" through the chambers and arteries made Sammy's understanding feel almost instinctual, as if he were seeing his own heart in action.

As exams approached, Sammy felt a confidence he hadn't expected. The glowing images stayed with him, like memories burned into his mind. With Blinky's help, he felt prepared and focused, ready to face whatever test questions came his way.

A Surprising Test Day

On the day of his big biology exam, Sammy walked into the lecture hall feeling calm and collected. He took a deep breath as he sat down, closing his eyes briefly to recall Blinky's glowing visuals. With each question, he could picture the scenes Blinky had created—the glowing cells, the chloroplasts, the heart pumping rhythmically in his mind's eye.

He moved through the exam with surprising ease, each answer feeling as if it were just waiting to be written. When he finished, he glanced at his backpack, feeling a quiet sense of gratitude.

Back in his dorm room that evening, Blinky beamed with pride as Sammy shared his test experience. "I think that's the best I've ever done on a biology exam," Sammy said, smiling. "I couldn't have done it without you, Blinky."

Blinky's glow softened with a hint of warmth. "You're the one who studied, Sammy. I just... made it a little brighter."

They shared a proud moment, and Sammy knew he was incredibly lucky to have a friend like Blinky. Not only had he become Sammy's personal note-taker, but he'd also turned learning into a vivid, unforgettable experience.

As they settled in for the night, Sammy found himself looking forward to his next lecture, knowing that with Blinky by his side, even the toughest subjects could be transformed into magical moments of discovery.

Chapter 11: The Magic of Meeting New People

Sammy had always thought of himself as fairly outgoing, but college felt like an entirely different world. Everywhere he turned, people were forming groups, introducing themselves, and diving into conversations with strangers. As much as he wanted to make new friends, he found it hard to know where to start.

One evening, he sat in his dorm room, scrolling through photos of student events on his phone, feeling a bit overwhelmed. "How do people just... click so easily?" he wondered aloud.

A soft voice answered him, barely louder than a whisper. "It's about finding a spark, Sammy. Like the magic you have with us," Mumbles said, emerging from a shadowy corner of the room.

Sammy smiled, grateful for the comforting presence of his monster friends. As if on cue, Whiffle, Blinky, and Munch appeared, each with their own ideas on how to help.

"You know, Sammy, making friends is just like any other adventure," Whiffle said with a cheerful grin. "You just have to be brave enough to take the first step!"

Blinky nodded, his glow warm and encouraging. "And remember, everyone's a little nervous. Sometimes a simple 'hello' is all it takes."

Munch, who had been quietly munching on a cookie, swallowed and added, "And snacks! People love snacks. Maybe bring some with you."

Sammy laughed, feeling his nerves start to fade. "I think you guys might be onto something. Maybe I just need to put myself out there a little more."

"Exactly!" Mumbles whispered. "And we'll be there to help if you need it."

That night, they made a plan. Sammy would go to the next student icebreaker event, and his monster friends would find subtle ways to lend him confidence, offering little nudges of support from the shadows.

The following evening, Sammy walked into the student lounge, where the icebreaker was being held. The room was bustling with activity, filled with students chatting in small groups. He took a deep breath, feeling a familiar flutter of nerves, but he could sense the reassuring presence of his friends close by.

Just as he was gathering the courage to join a group, Whiffle whispered from behind him, "That group over there looks friendly. The one by the snack table."

Sammy glanced over and saw a small group of students laughing as they discussed their favorite foods. Following Whiffle's advice, he approached them, introduced himself, and soon found himself joining the conversation.

"Cookies are the ultimate comfort food," he chimed in, thinking of Munch's constant snacking. His comment earned a few laughs, and the group welcomed him easily, talking about their favorite snacks and the best places to grab a quick bite around campus.

As the evening continued, Sammy found himself facing another round of introductions. This time, Blinky offered some advice from his spot in Sammy's backpack. "Ask questions, Sammy! People love talking about themselves. It helps them feel at ease."

Taking Blinky's advice to heart, Sammy turned to a nearby student named Maya and asked, "So, Maya, what's something you're excited to do in college?"

Maya's face lit up, and she started talking about her plans to join the photography club. As she shared her enthusiasm for capturing candid moments, Sammy felt himself relaxing, realizing that connecting with people was easier than he'd thought. Blinky's advice had been spot on.

Just as Sammy was starting to feel more confident, the group leader announced a new activity: everyone was to form pairs and come up with three fun facts about themselves to share with the room.

Sammy's nerves returned momentarily as he glanced around, but before he could overthink it, Mumbles' whisper filled his ear. "Be yourself, Sammy. You have amazing stories."

With Mumbles' encouragement, Sammy partnered with a student named Leo, who looked just as nervous as he felt. As they talked, Sammy shared a fun fact about his love for mystery novels and how he used to create "detective cases" with his friends back home. Leo's face lit up, saying he loved mysteries too.

By the time they presented their facts, Sammy realized he'd found a shared interest—and maybe even a potential friend. He felt a rush of gratitude for Mumbles' reminder to stay true to himself.

After the activity, Munch decided to step in with his own kind of support. He sneaked out a small stash of treats from Sammy's backpack and whispered, "Offer them a snack, Sammy. Everyone loves a little surprise treat."

Sammy chuckled and offered a few of the cookies Munch had snuck in. The gesture sparked another round of laughter and conversation, with people talking about their favorite snacks and family recipes. The simple act of sharing made Sammy feel more at ease, and he noticed that people around him seemed to relax as well.

By the end of the evening, Sammy felt a warmth that he hadn't expected. His monster friends' advice had been small, subtle, but powerful. Whiffle's reminder to take the first step, Blinky's advice on asking questions, Mumbles' encouragement to be himself, and Munch's idea to share snacks had each helped him connect with others in different ways.

As he walked back to his dorm room, Sammy's heart felt lighter. He knew that he'd made the first few connections he'd been hoping for, and he owed it to the magical wisdom of his monster friends.

When he reached his room, they appeared around him, each one beaming with pride.

"You did amazing, Sammy!" Whiffle cheered, bouncing with excitement. "Look at all the friends you made!"

Sammy grinned. "Thanks to you guys. I couldn't have done it without your advice."

Blinky floated up, glowing warmly. "You had it in you all along, Sammy. We just gave you a little boost."

Munch gave him a friendly pat on the back, handing him one last cookie as a reward. "Just remember, every friend you make is another person to share snacks with."

They all laughed, sharing a quiet moment of joy. Sammy realized that he was lucky to have his monster friends by his side, not only for their magical tricks and fun but for the way they truly understood him.

As he got ready for bed, Sammy felt a sense of excitement for the friendships and memories still to come. Thanks to his friends' guidance, he was ready to meet new people, share new experiences, and keep exploring the magic of college life.

Chapter 12: The College Costume Party

A few weeks into the semester, Sammy's dorm was abuzz with talk about the upcoming college costume party. Flyers had been pinned up everywhere, announcing it as the biggest social event of the month. Students were planning elaborate outfits, and Sammy could already hear his friends discussing their costume ideas in the halls.

One evening, Sammy returned to his dorm room to find his monster friends waiting, each with a mischievous glint in their eyes. Munch, Whiffle, Blinky, and Mumbles had all gathered, and it was clear they were up to something.

"Sammy!" Whiffle exclaimed, bouncing with excitement. "We heard there's a costume party happening, and we have the perfect idea."

Sammy raised an eyebrow, intrigued. "Oh? Let's hear it."

Blinky's glow brightened as he grinned. "You're going as one of us—a magical monster! And we'll each add our special touch to make sure you're the best-dressed monster at the party."

Sammy chuckled, already loving the idea. "Alright, I'm in. So, what kind of magical monster are we creating?"

Mumbles leaned in, his voice soft but enthusiastic. "A blend of all our best qualities. Think glow, sparkle, and a little bit of mystery."

Sammy could hardly contain his excitement. Together, they brainstormed the ultimate monster-inspired costume, incorporating elements from each of his friends.

Creating the Monster Look

On the night of the party, Sammy and his friends gathered all the materials they could find—pieces of old fabric, face paint, and an assortment of small props. Whiffle took charge of crafting the base of the costume, helping Sammy create a set of furry, glitter-dusted shoulder pads that shimmered with every movement.

"These will make you look both fierce and fluffy," Whiffle said, dusting Sammy's shoulders with a hint of blue glitter. "Plus, you'll leave a sparkly trail wherever you go!"

Next, Blinky added his touch. He held out a few small, glowing stones he'd found and arranged them on Sammy's costume, each one twinkling like a tiny star. "These are enchanted stones," he explained with a smile. "They'll glow faintly and make you look like you're covered in stardust."

Sammy marvelled at the effect. The glowing stones cast a gentle, mysterious light, adding an otherworldly quality to his look.

Munch, who was always full of surprises, pulled out a small, old bag filled with glitter and colorful confetti. "This is for the big entrance," he said with a wink. "Whenever you walk into a room, toss a little of this. It'll be like your own mini celebration."

Finally, Mumbles added the finishing touch: he gently painted faint, swirling patterns across Sammy's face and arms with invisible ink. When Sammy held up a small blacklight that Blinky provided, the ink glowed faintly, creating mysterious, ghostly patterns. Mumbles whispered, "This will only be visible when you want it to be. Just a little mystery for the right moments."

By the time they were finished, Sammy looked like a creature from a magical realm—glittering shoulders, glowing stones, swirling patterns, and a small pouch of confetti at his side. He gazed at himself in the mirror, amazed by the transformation.

"This is incredible, you guys," he said, smiling at each of his friends. "I feel like... well, one of you."

Whiffle beamed. "That's the idea! Now, go show everyone what a magical monster looks like!"

The Grand Entrance

When Sammy arrived at the party, heads turned immediately. Students were dressed as superheroes, pirates, and historical figures, but Sammy's monster-inspired look stood out in a sea of costumes.

As he stepped into the room, he tossed a handful of Munch's glittery confetti into the air, creating a sparkling burst that caught the light and fell around him like magic dust. The glow from Blinky's enchanted stones added an ethereal quality, and with each step, the glitter from his shoulder pads trailed softly behind him.

People watched in awe, wondering who he was supposed to be. Some thought he might be an alien, while others whispered about him being a creature from a fantasy novel. Sammy smiled, enjoying the mystery his costume was creating.

A group of students came over, one of them asking, "Whoa, who are you supposed to be?"

Sammy grinned, giving a small bow. "Just a creature from another world," he replied with a wink, deciding to keep the magic alive.

A Magical Time with New Friends

As the night went on, Sammy found himself meeting new people who were intrigued by his look. The mystery of his costume seemed to invite conversations, and he spent the night chatting with students he hadn't met before, sharing stories and laughing as they tried to guess what he was dressed as.

Emma and Liam, his friends from the Secret Club, eventually found him and marvelled at his outfit.

"This is the best costume here!" Emma said, examining the glowing stones on his costume. "It's like you brought a piece of the stars with you."

Sammy chuckled. "Maybe I did. A few friends helped me out with it."

Liam grinned. "Well, whoever they are, they did a fantastic job."

Throughout the night, Sammy's monster friends found small, creative ways to join in the fun. Whenever he entered a dark corner of the room, Mumbles made the invisible ink patterns on Sammy's face and arms glow faintly, adding a spooky, ghostly effect that made people gasp with wonder. Whiffle occasionally added a quick sprinkle of glitter from Sammy's shoulder pads, ensuring that he left a trail of sparkle wherever he went.

At one point, Munch even tossed a handful of confetti when Sammy wasn't looking, surprising everyone around him with a sudden burst of colorful magic.

A Night to Remember

As the party wound down, Sammy realized he'd spent the evening laughing and talking more than he had at any other event since starting college. His costume, with all its magical touches, had made him feel confident and free, allowing him to connect with others in a way he hadn't expected.

He found a quiet corner near the end of the night, and his friends gathered around him, each one beaming with pride.

"You were the hit of the party, Sammy!" Whiffle said, giving him a playful nudge. "Didn't I tell you the costume would work?"

Sammy laughed. "You were right, Whiffle. I've never felt more... myself."

Blinky's glow softened as he floated closer. "It's not just the costume, Sammy. It's the magic of being yourself—and a little mystery."

Mumbles whispered, "Sometimes, all it takes is a little sparkle."

Munch handed him one last cookie from the party, patting him on the back. "You're one of us, Sammy. Always have been."

With a grateful smile, Sammy took a bite of the cookie, savouring the moment. He knew this night would be one he'd remember for a long time—a night filled with laughter, magic, and the comforting knowledge that his friends would always be by his side, helping him shine in his own unique way.

As he walked back to his dorm, the faint glow of his costume lighting the way, Sammy couldn't help but feel grateful. College might be filled with challenges, but with friends like his, each new experience held the potential for a little magic and a lot of unforgettable memories.

Chapter 13: A Monster-Made Study Guide

Finals were around the corner, and Sammy's dorm room had turned into a fortress of textbooks, notes, and highlighters. His desk was buried in paper, and every inch of space seemed to be covered in study material. Despite all his preparations, Sammy couldn't shake the feeling of being overwhelmed by the sheer volume of information he had to review.

One evening, as he stared at a page of biology notes, exhausted, his friends materialized around him, each of them wearing expressions of determination—and a hint of mischief.

"Sammy, it's time for a study guide," Whiffle declared, looking at the piles of notes with a discerning eye. "But not just any study guide," he added, glancing at the others with a grin.

Blinky's glow brightened as he grinned back. "We're making you the ultimate Monster-Made Study Guide!"

Munch tossed a handful of crackers into his mouth and gave Sammy a thumbs-up. "We'll make sure you're prepared, Sammy. And don't worry—it'll be fun."

Sammy laughed, curiosity mixing with relief. "Alright, let's see what you've got!"

The monsters quickly got to work, organizing Sammy's notes and creating the most magical, interactive study guide he'd ever seen.

Biology: A Living Diagram

Blinky took the lead on biology, hovering over Sammy's notes on human anatomy. With a wave of his glowing hand, he transformed the flat diagrams on the page into living, floating images. Cells pulsed gently in mid-air, tiny organelles moved like dancers in a cosmic ballet, and each part of the cell glowed in different colors.

As Sammy watched, Blinky highlighted the nucleus in a warm glow. "Think of the nucleus as the brain of the cell," he explained, making it sparkle for emphasis. "Just like your brain helps you think, the nucleus controls everything that happens in here."

Munch couldn't resist adding a snack-related analogy. "It's like the control room of a giant snack factory," he said, grinning. "The nucleus decides what kind of cookies—uh, proteins—the cell needs to make."

Sammy chuckled, imagining cells as tiny snack factories. The image stuck, and as he took notes, he realized he'd remember this quirky analogy long after the test was over.

Chemistry: Glowing Reactions

For chemistry, Blinky stepped up again, this time using his glow to illustrate different chemical reactions. He began by projecting simple molecules in the air, showing how atoms bonded and separated.

When they reached the section on combustion, Blinky created a small, harmless "flame" effect, making the molecules burst apart and recombine with a magical flare. Sammy couldn't help but marvel at how easy it was to understand now that he could actually see the reactions.

"Here's the trick," Blinky explained, creating a mini fireworks show. "Remember the molecules are like dance partners. In a reaction, they change partners, and sometimes, like in combustion, they create a big showy result."

Mumbles added, "Just remember the right balance of atoms in each dance. Too many partners, and the dance falls apart."

Sammy nodded, amazed at how much more chemistry made sense when Blinky turned each reaction into a glowing, animated performance.

History: The Hilarious Timeline

Whiffle took on the task of helping Sammy with history, using a touch of humour to make the timeline come alive. He created a floating timeline in the air, with each event marked by a tiny caricature that he'd carefully crafted.

At each point on the timeline, little figures reenacted historical events with exaggerated expressions and silly sound effects. Kings and queens waved dramatically, knights clanked around with oversized swords, and inventors danced as they held up lightbulbs.

"See?" Whiffle said, laughing. "History doesn't have to be boring. Imagine each leader as a character. Like here—King Henry VIII," he said, making a tiny Henry wave a giant turkey leg. "He's the guy who changed things up just because he wanted a new wife!"

Sammy burst out laughing, the mental image cementing the event in his mind. Whiffle's humour turned each historical moment into a scene he could easily recall, and Sammy found himself memorizing dates and details without even realizing it.

Math: The Snack Problem

Munch volunteered for math, naturally adding his own snack-themed twist. He took Sammy's notes on calculus and started drawing snack-related examples all over the page. Limits and derivatives became easy to grasp when Munch turned them into food puzzles.

"For example," Munch said, drawing a curve with tiny crackers along it, "think of derivatives as the snack consumption rate. How fast are you eating these crackers at any given point on the curve?"

He munched a cracker to emphasize his point, and Sammy couldn't help but laugh. "So derivatives are like... my snacking speed?"

"Exactly!" Munch grinned. "And integrals? That's just figuring out the total number of snacks you ate."

With each equation, Munch found a way to work in a snack analogy, and by the end, Sammy could recall each concept clearly—probably because he'd also managed to munch through half a bag of crackers along the way.

English Literature: A Dramatic Reading

Mumbles took on English literature, his whispery voice adding an air of mystery to each story. He started with Shakespeare, reading in a soft, ghostly tone that made each line sound more captivating than ever before.

As he recited, he created floating, ghostly images of the characters: Hamlet contemplating his skull, Macbeth gripping a blood-stained dagger, and Juliet leaning over her balcony. Mumbles' dramatic whispers made each scene feel alive, as if Sammy were watching a ghostly play unfold in front of him.

"Remember, Sammy," Mumbles whispered, "these characters have emotions. Imagine what each one is feeling, and you'll understand the story better."

Sammy listened intently, enchanted by Mumbles' performance. Each scene stuck with him, and by the end of the night, he could easily recount the major themes of each story.

A Quiz with a Twist

After hours of reviewing with their animated study guide, the monsters decided to give Sammy a little quiz to test his knowledge. Each friend took a turn asking him questions, using their unique tricks to add fun to the process.

Whiffle used his timeline for history questions, while Blinky created molecule puzzles for chemistry. Munch tossed Sammy snack-related math problems, and Mumbles challenged him with dramatic literature questions, whispering clues if he struggled.

As they quizzed him, Sammy found himself laughing, remembering each lesson with perfect clarity. He was amazed at how much information he had absorbed through their quirky study guide, and by the time they were done, he felt more confident than ever.

A Heartfelt Thank-You

The night before his finals, Sammy sat with his friends, feeling a mixture of gratitude and excitement. "You guys... you're incredible. I couldn't have done this without you."

Whiffle grinned, throwing a bit of glitter in the air. "We knew you had it in you, Sammy! We just added a bit of monster magic."

Blinky's glow softened. "And a little light to make things clear."

Mumbles gave him a gentle smile. "Remember, Sammy, you've got all the knowledge in you. We just made it a bit... memorable."

Munch handed him one last cracker for good luck. "And don't forget to snack during the test. Keeps the brain sharp!"

Sammy chuckled, feeling a warm sense of pride and friendship. He knew that no matter what the tests held, he had the best support team anyone could ask for.

Chapter 14: The Glittery Graduation Dream

It was late, and Sammy was exhausted after a long night of studying. Finals were nearly over, and the anticipation of finishing his first year at college filled him with excitement. As he lay in bed, his thoughts drifted to the future, to the moment when he would walk across the stage at graduation, diploma in hand, ready for whatever life had in store.

With these thoughts swirling in his mind, Sammy slowly drifted off to sleep, slipping into a deep, comforting dream.

In the dream, he was standing in a massive, sunlit auditorium. Rows of seats stretched out in every direction, filled with cheering faces. But what struck him most was the stage itself. There, lined up proudly, were his monster friends, each one dressed in a unique cap and gown, eagerly waiting for him to join them.

Sammy's heart swelled with happiness as he took in the sight. Whiffle, Blinky, Mumbles, and Munch were all wearing caps adorned with glitter, tassels, and symbols of their personalities. They looked as excited as he felt, each one giving him a little wave or thumbs-up.

Whiffle's Glittery Ensemble

Whiffle's cap and gown sparkled under the bright lights, covered in shimmering glitter that seemed to float off him in little puffs. His cap was adorned with a tiny tassel shaped like a star, and he wore a massive grin as he waved excitedly at Sammy.

"Sammy!" Whiffle called out, his voice ringing through the auditorium. "Can you believe we made it to graduation? We've been through so many adventures together!"

Sammy couldn't help but laugh. "I know, Whiffle! And look at you—you're the sparkiest graduate here!"

Whiffle did a little spin, leaving a trail of glitter that sparkled in the air. "Only the best for our special day," he said proudly.

Blinky's Glowing Attire

Blinky stood next to Whiffle, his cap and gown glowing with a soft, otherworldly light. His cap was decorated with tiny lights that twinkled like stars, and his gown shifted colors as he moved, casting a gentle, warm glow.

When Sammy approached, Blinky extended a glowing hand and gave him a proud smile. "Congratulations, Sammy. You've worked so hard, and we're all so proud of you."

"Thanks, Blinky," Sammy said, feeling a lump in his throat. "I couldn't have done it without you."

Blinky's glow brightened for a moment. "We've all been with you every step of the way. This is your day, Sammy, but it's our celebration too."

Mumbles' Ghostly Graduation Look

Mumbles' gown was a soft, ethereal grey, almost translucent, and his cap floated just above his head, faintly shimmering in and out of view. His tassel seemed to have a life of its own, drifting lazily from side to side.

When Sammy reached him, Mumbles gave him a quiet smile and whispered, "You've always been part of our world, Sammy. Now, seeing you here makes everything feel complete."

Sammy bent down to hug him, feeling the warmth of his friend's spirit. "Thanks, Mumbles. I'll never forget any of this."

Mumbles patted Sammy's shoulder. "You carry a little piece of us with you, no matter where you go."

Munch's Snack-Filled Graduation Gown

Munch, true to form, had accessorized his cap and gown with tiny snack bags sewn along the edges, each one labelled with different treats he'd shared with Sammy over the years. His tassel was shaped like a cookie, and he grinned from ear to ear as he handed Sammy a small bag of crackers.

"Congratulations, Sammy!" Munch said, stuffing a cracker into his mouth. "This is a big deal, so I made sure to bring a little feast for our special day."

Sammy laughed, taking the snack with gratitude. "Thanks, Munch. I knew I could count on you to bring the party snacks."

Munch gave him a playful nudge. "Hey, every celebration needs a little snack magic!"

A Glorious Graduation Ceremony

As Sammy stood with his friends, he noticed other graduates filling the seats behind them—students, teachers, and even family members who had been part of his journey. Everyone was smiling, clapping, and cheering as he took his place on stage.

Then, a voice echoed through the auditorium, announcing his name. Sammy took a deep breath, feeling the warmth of his friends surrounding him as he stepped forward. In his dream, his diploma floated toward him, glittering in the same magical light that had followed him since he'd first met his monster friends.

As he held the diploma in his hands, Sammy looked back at Whiffle, Blinky, Mumbles, and Munch, each one beaming with pride.

"We're so proud of you, Sammy!" they cheered in unison, their voices filling the air with joy and excitement.

Just as the crowd's applause began to fade, Whiffle stepped forward, reaching into a hidden pocket of his gown. With a wink, he tossed a handful of glitter into the air, creating a sparkling cloud that floated around Sammy and his friends. The glitter caught the light, swirling around them like a magical confetti shower, each piece reflecting the memories they had shared together.

The Heartfelt Goodbye

As the ceremony continued, Sammy's heart swelled with gratitude, realizing that this wasn't just a graduation—it was a celebration of everything he had learned, both from his classes and from the friends who had been with him every step of the way.

In that moment, he felt a deep sense of peace, knowing that his monster friends would always be with him, even as he moved forward into new chapters of his life.

"Thank you, all of you," he said, his voice filled with emotion. "I'll never forget the magic we've shared."

Each of his friends reached out, wrapping him in a warm, comforting embrace. And as the glitter continued to drift around them, Sammy knew he was ready for whatever came next.

Waking Up

Sammy awoke with a peaceful smile, the dream still vivid in his mind. He looked around his dorm room, feeling the comforting presence of his friends, even if they weren't physically there at that moment.

Later that day, as he shared the details of his dream with Whiffle, Blinky, Mumbles, and Munch, they listened with wide smiles and shining eyes, each one touched by the thought of his dream graduation.

"It was like you were really there with me," Sammy said, grinning. "And I wouldn't have it any other way."

Whiffle gave a proud nod, dusting a little glitter onto Sammy's shoulder. "When the day comes, we'll be there, Sammy. And it'll be just as magical as you dreamed."

Blinky glowed brightly, Mumbles gave a warm, quiet smile, and Munch handed him a snack for good measure. Sammy felt a wave of gratitude wash over him, knowing that no matter where life took him, he'd always have the magic of his monster friends in his heart.

And as he prepared for the final days of his semester, Sammy knew that he was ready to face anything, with a little monster magic by his side, now and forever.

Chapter 15: The Nighttime Lab Experiment

It was a quiet evening on campus, and Sammy was winding down after a long day of classes. His homework was done, his roommate was off studying with friends, and the dorm was unusually quiet. Sammy was just about to settle into bed when Blinky appeared, his soft blue glow lighting up the room.

"Sammy," Blinky whispered with an excited glint in his eyes, "how would you like to see a little nighttime science magic?"

Sammy's curiosity was instantly piqued. "What do you have in mind?"

Blinky's glow brightened. "I've been watching the chemistry professor's lectures, and I've learned a thing or two about... well, let's just say some 'unexplored applications' of lab materials. The science building is empty now—it's the perfect time to try a few fun experiments!"

Sammy grinned, already reaching for his hoodie. He knew better than to turn down an adventure with Blinky. "Lead the way, Professor Blinky."

Entering the Lab

They snuck across campus under the cover of darkness, slipping into the science building through a side door Blinky had conveniently "unlocked" with a little glow-enhanced nudge. The lab was quiet and dimly lit, with rows of test tubes, beakers, and mysterious chemicals lining the shelves.

Sammy felt a thrill of excitement. "Alright, Blinky. What's first on the experiment list?"

Blinky floated over to a counter, his glow illuminating a set of flasks filled with colorful liquids. "We'll start with something simple—let's mix a few harmless chemicals and see if we can make them... glow."

With a nod, Sammy picked up a flask filled with a blue liquid, carefully pouring it into a beaker that Blinky held steady. As the liquids combined, Blinky's glow intensified, causing the mixture to emit a faint, eerie light.

"Look at that!" Sammy whispered, amazed. The blue liquid shimmered in the dark, swirling with a ghostly glow that matched Blinky's own light.

But before they could admire it further, the mixture started bubbling, fizzing more than they'd expected. The bubbles grew larger and began popping, releasing little clouds of glittery mist into the air.

Blinky chuckled. "Well, that was unexpected... but I think it adds a nice touch!"

The Sparkling Reaction

Emboldened by their first success, Blinky floated over to a set of powdered chemicals in small, labelled jars. "I heard the professor say something about 'exothermic reactions' the other day. Let's give it a try—just a tiny one!"

They mixed a small amount of powder into another beaker of liquid, and almost immediately, the solution began to sparkle. Tiny sparks danced across the surface, giving off a faint crackling sound, like a mini firework show contained in glass.

Sammy's eyes widened. "Blinky, this is amazing! It's like a science show just for us!"

The sparkles continued to flicker, but as they settled down, a faint, pleasant smell filled the air, like sweet lavender mixed with a hint of citrus.

Blinky hovered over the beaker, looking pleased. "I may have added a tiny pinch of lavender powder for fun," he admitted. "Science doesn't always have to smell like chemicals!"

Sammy laughed, inhaling the pleasant scent. He had to admit, Blinky's approach to chemistry was much more enjoyable than anything he'd done in class.

The Unintended Slime Explosion

Their experiments continued, with Sammy and Blinky trying out various harmless mixtures, each one creating its own unique reaction. But it wasn't long before curiosity got the better of them, and they decided to try something a little more... daring.

They found a jar labelled "Sodium Alginate" and another marked "Calcium Chloride." Blinky's eyes sparkled with excitement as he whispered, "This could make something squishy. Let's make our own lab slime!"

They carefully measured out small amounts, mixing them together with water. The liquid thickened almost immediately, turning into a gooey, stretchy blob. Sammy poked it, laughing at the slimy texture, but as he did, the blob expanded, growing larger and wobbling in the beaker.

Before they could react, the slime grew so much that it overflowed the container, spilling onto the counter and dripping onto the floor in large, squishy globs.

"Uh... Blinky?" Sammy asked, his voice filled with both awe and a bit of panic. "I think we made... too much slime."

Blinky laughed, floating back as the blob continued to grow. "Quick! Grab the baking soda—it should help solidify it."

They scrambled, grabbing supplies and managing to halt the slime's growth with a generous dusting of baking soda. The resulting mess covered the counter in stretchy, slightly glittery slime, but the crisis was averted.

Wiping slime off his hands, Sammy couldn't stop laughing. "That was... way more than I expected, but that might've been the most fun I've ever had with chemistry."

The Glowing Volcano

After cleaning up the slime explosion, Blinky suggested they try one last experiment. He floated over to a small bottle labelled "Vinegar" and another filled with baking soda, grinning.

"Ready for a classic?" he asked, his glow flickering in excitement.

Sammy nodded, recognizing the ingredients for a classic vinegar-and-baking-soda volcano. But Blinky had a twist—he added a pinch of phosphorescent powder to the baking soda, giving the mixture a slight glow.

They piled the baking soda in a beaker, then poured the vinegar in, watching as the foamy reaction erupted in a glowing, bubbling volcano. The foam poured over the edges, glowing faintly in the dim light, and Sammy couldn't stop smiling.

"This is incredible," he said, watching the glowing foam spread across the counter. "We've turned the lab into a mini science carnival!"

A Close Call

Just as they were admiring their glowing volcano, they heard footsteps echoing down the hall. Sammy's eyes widened in panic.

"Uh-oh! Someone's coming!" he whispered.

Without missing a beat, Blinky dimmed his glow and quickly flew to the door, nudging it closed just enough to keep their activities hidden. They hurriedly cleaned up the remaining mess, wiping down the counters and shoving containers back onto shelves.

The footsteps grew louder, pausing outside the lab door. Sammy held his breath, heart pounding, as he and Blinky stood frozen in the dim light. But after a few tense seconds, the footsteps moved on, fading into the distance.

Blinky let out a soft laugh. "Looks like we almost had a visitor! Good thing we didn't leave too much slime behind."

Sammy exhaled in relief, grinning. "Yeah, I don't think 'midnight slime experiment' would go over well with campus staff."

A Magical Conclusion

With the coast clear, Sammy and Blinky finished tidying up, careful to leave no trace of their nighttime science adventure. As they slipped back out of the lab, Sammy looked back, feeling a strange sense of satisfaction. He knew they hadn't followed traditional lab protocols, but this was the most excited he'd ever felt about science.

As they made their way back to the dorm, Sammy turned to Blinky, giving him a grateful smile. "Thanks, Blinky. Tonight was... well, it was magical."

Blinky glowed softly, his smile warm and content. "Anytime, Sammy. Science has a kind of magic all its own. Sometimes, all it takes is a little glow to bring it to life."

Sammy nodded, feeling a sense of wonder he hadn't expected. He realized that with friends like Blinky, even the most ordinary things—like lab experiments—could become extraordinary adventures.

As he crawled into bed that night, Sammy felt a quiet thrill. Finals and assignments could be tough, but thanks to Blinky, he had a whole new appreciation for chemistry. And as he drifted off to sleep, he wondered what other secrets the campus held, just waiting for a little nighttime magic to bring them to life.

Chapter 16: Roommate Rescue

Sammy returned to his dorm room one evening to find his roommate, Jake, slouched at his desk, looking utterly defeated. Papers were scattered everywhere, his books were piled high, and a long, loud sigh escaped him as he buried his face in his hands.

"Hey, Jake. You okay?" Sammy asked, setting down his backpack.

Jake shook his head, mumbling, "It's just... one of those days, man. Everything's piling up—classes, work, and now I can't find my project notes, and... I'm just done."

Seeing his usually upbeat roommate looking so down was unusual, and Sammy's heart went out to him. Jake was always the one who cracked jokes and lifted everyone's spirits. Sammy knew he couldn't fix Jake's problems, but he could try to make his day a little brighter.

As he pondered what to do, Whiffle, Blinky, Munch, and Mumbles appeared, each one looking determined.

"We heard what happened," Whiffle said, his fur sparkling with extra glitter. "And we're going to cheer him up—monster-style!"

Blinky's glow softened. "Everyone needs a little light on tough days. Let's give Jake a small reminder that things can get better."

Sammy smiled, knowing that with his monster friends, they could turn any bad day around. "Alright, team. Let's do this."

A Trail of Glitter and Surprises

The monsters quickly set their plan into motion, starting with a simple but magical touch—a trail of glitter leading from Jake's desk to his bed. Whiffle sprinkled his signature blue and silver glitter around, making a shimmering path that caught the light and looked like something out of a dream.

Jake, still looking miserable, finally noticed the sparkling trail. He raised his head and stared at it in confusion.

"Uh... Sammy, is there a reason there's glitter all over the floor?" Jake asked, managing a small, curious smile.

Sammy shrugged nonchalantly, trying to hide his grin. "I dunno, Jake. Maybe it's a little bit of magic."

Jake rolled his eyes but couldn't help laughing a bit. As he got up to follow the trail, the glitter led him to his bed, where Munch had left a small bag of Jake's favorite snacks—pretzels, peanut butter cups, and a note that read:

"A snack for every worry. One bite at a time, Jake!"

Jake chuckled, picking up a peanut butter cup. "Okay, I admit, this is kinda nice."

Munch peeked out from behind the bed, giving Sammy a thumbs-up as he munched on his own treat.

A Glow of Encouragement

Next, Blinky floated over to Jake's desk, where his stack of books loomed intimidatingly. He glowed gently, creating a warm light that illuminated the books and cast a calming glow across Jake's workspace.

As Jake sat back down, he noticed the unusual, comforting glow. "Did you do something to the lights, Sammy? This feels... peaceful."

Sammy shrugged, giving Blinky a grateful nod. "Maybe it's just a bit of encouragement, Jake. You've got this."

Blinky added a soft, pulsing light to the corner of Jake's computer, making it feel like there was a supportive little glow cheering him on. Jake smiled as he returned to his work, seeming a bit more at ease.

Invisible Ink Messages from Mumbles

Meanwhile, Mumbles went to work with his invisible ink, leaving small, hidden messages on Jake's notes and around his desk. He wrote words of encouragement and funny little drawings that only revealed themselves under a specific light.

As Jake picked up one of his notes, he noticed faint glowing letters appear across the page: "You're stronger than you think."

He blinked in surprise, holding up another paper, where a tiny doodle of a stick figure giving a thumbs-up emerged. Each page had a different message—"You can do this," "One thing at a time," and "Believe in yourself."

Jake's smile widened with each new message, and he looked up at Sammy, eyebrows raised. "Did you leave these for me?"

Sammy gave a small shrug, trying to keep a straight face. "Maybe I had a little help."

"Either way," Jake said, chuckling, "I feel a lot better already. Thanks, man."

The Cozy Blanket Fort

Whiffle, wanting to make Jake feel truly comfortable, gathered up spare blankets and pillows from Sammy's closet and started constructing a cozy blanket fort in the corner of the room. By the time he was done, it was a little haven of comfort, with fairy lights draped around the edges and a soft pile of pillows in the middle.

Jake noticed the fort and grinned. "A blanket fort? Seriously, Sammy?"

"Nothing like a little childhood magic," Sammy replied. "You'd be surprised how good it feels to curl up in there."

With a laugh, Jake crawled into the fort, resting against the pillows as the fairy lights twinkled softly around him. Whiffle sprinkled a bit more glitter for extra magic, giving the fort a gentle, dreamlike quality.

As Jake relaxed in the fort, he glanced over at Sammy, his face relaxed and his earlier frustration melting away. "You know, this actually makes me feel a lot better. It's like... I'm a kid again, when things were simpler."

Whiffle beamed, happy to have helped.

A Thoughtful Ending with Mumbles

Finally, Mumbles drifted over to Jake, who was now comfortably snuggled in the fort, and whispered softly to him, "Just remember, Jake—tomorrow is a new day. Today's worries don't have to be tomorrow's."

Jake, half-asleep, looked up as if he had heard a gentle breeze. The words sank in, filling him with a sense of peace and calm. He lay back against the pillows, smiling softly.

Mumbles floated back to Sammy, giving a satisfied nod. "I think we've done our job."

A Room Filled with Kindness

By the time Sammy's monsters had finished, the dorm room was transformed. Glitter shimmered on the floor, snacks and encouraging notes were scattered around, and the blanket fort stood as a cozy sanctuary. The atmosphere was warm and filled with the quiet magic of friendship.

Jake looked around, a grateful expression on his face. "Sammy, I don't know how you pulled this off, but... thank you. I really needed this."

Sammy smiled, glad that his friend was feeling better. "Sometimes, we all just need a little kindness."

Jake settled back into the fort, enjoying his snacks and the comforting light from Blinky. Sammy watched as Jake's stress dissolved, replaced by a quiet sense of calm and contentment.

As his monsters gave him a quiet thumbs-up from the shadows, Sammy felt his heart swell with pride and gratitude. Knowing that he could bring a bit of magic to Jake's day was the best feeling he could ask for.

And as the night went on, Sammy knew that with friends like these, even the toughest days could be met with kindness, laughter, and a little bit of monster magic.

Chapter 17: The Phantom of the Cafeteria

It all started when Sammy's monster friend Munch discovered the concept of an "all-you-can-eat" meal plan. For Munch, who was always on the hunt for snacks, the very idea of unlimited food was like a dream come true. Sammy had casually mentioned the meal plan to Munch one day, not realizing the consequences this would have.

"So... you're telling me there's a place on campus where food is limitless?" Munch asked, his eyes widening with excitement.

Sammy chuckled. "Well, kind of! It's in the cafeteria, but that's only during the day. You can't just walk in whenever you want."

Munch's face fell slightly, but his eyes still sparkled with mischief. "Only during the day, huh? Sounds like a challenge to me."

Sammy raised an eyebrow, knowing that look all too well. "Munch, don't even think about it."

But that night, while Sammy was fast asleep, Munch's curiosity—and his appetite—got the better of him.

The First Midnight Feast

The cafeteria was dark and silent when Munch snuck in, his tiny frame barely making a sound. With his quick and stealthy moves, he slipped in through an unlocked side door, the promise of food drawing him in like a magnet.

In the dim light, Munch found himself surrounded by stacks of bread, trays of muffins, bowls of fruit, and even the leftovers of pasta and pizza from dinner. His eyes gleamed with excitement as he filled a plate with a little of everything.

As he munched away, he couldn't help but hum a little tune, his contentment echoing through the empty cafeteria. Between bites, he darted from table to table, grabbing a cookie here, a bagel there, nibbling his way through a late-night buffet.

By the time he was finished, Munch was happily stuffed, crumbs scattered around his mouth. He cleaned up as best as he could, leaving only a few stray crumbs behind, and quietly slipped out into the night.

The First Sighting of the "Phantom Diner"

The next day, Sammy overheard students talking about a strange discovery.

"Did you hear?" one student whispered. "Apparently, the cafeteria staff found food all over the place this morning. It's like someone had a feast after hours."

"Yeah," another added. "And they're calling it the 'Phantom of the Cafeteria.' Some say they even heard weird noises, like someone humming."

Sammy's eyes widened. Could it be? He had a sneaking suspicion about who the "phantom" might be.

Later that evening, he confronted Munch in their dorm room. "Munch, you wouldn't happen to know anything about this 'phantom diner,' would you?"

Munch grinned sheepishly, crumbs still clinging to his fur. "Uh... maybe?"

Sammy sighed, but he couldn't help laughing. "Munch, you can't just sneak into the cafeteria! People are starting to talk!"

Munch shrugged, his eyes twinkling. "But Sammy, it's an all-you-can-eat plan! And besides, I was careful. Mostly..."

The "Phantom" Returns

Despite Sammy's warnings, Munch couldn't resist the allure of the cafeteria's bounty. The very next night, he returned, slipping in through a different entrance this time, determined to be more discreet.

He tiptoed through the darkened kitchen, selecting only his favorite snacks—apple turnovers, mini sandwiches, and a few chocolate chip cookies for dessert. But his enthusiasm got the better of him, and he hummed happily as he ate, the sound echoing off the empty walls.

Unbeknownst to Munch, a custodian working late heard the humming and glimpsed a small, shadowy figure darting through the cafeteria. The custodian only caught a quick flash of movement, but it was enough to spark more rumours the next day.

The Campus Buzz

By now, the "Phantom of the Cafeteria" had become a full-blown campus legend. Students shared stories of late-night snack bandits and "mysterious diners" who roamed the cafeteria after hours.

Some students claimed they had heard strange noises coming from the cafeteria at night, and others swore they'd seen footprints (left, no doubt, by Munch's messy escapades). The story took on a life of its own, with each retelling adding a layer of mystery and intrigue.

One morning, Sammy overheard a group of students talking excitedly. "Did you hear? They say the phantom eats like a monster, leaving trails of crumbs and snack wrappers everywhere!"

Another student added, "I even heard they leave behind glowing crumbs!"

Sammy knew he had to intervene before the situation got out of hand.

A Midnight Stakeout

Determined to put a stop to Munch's midnight feasts, Sammy hatched a plan. That night, he waited until Munch was asleep, then snuck out to the cafeteria himself, hiding in a corner where he could observe any "phantom" activity.

Sure enough, around midnight, he heard soft footsteps and a faint humming sound. Munch slipped in through the side door, his eyes gleaming as he made a beeline for the dessert counter. As he reached for a slice of pie, Sammy stepped out of the shadows.

"Munch," he whispered, crossing his arms.

Munch froze, pie slice in hand, his eyes wide with surprise. "Uh… Sammy! Fancy seeing you here."

Sammy sighed, trying to keep a straight face. "Munch, we have to put an end to this. You're becoming a campus legend!"

Munch's face lit up with pride. "A legend, huh?"

Sammy shook his head, smiling despite himself. "But not exactly the kind of legend we want! Besides, you're going to get caught eventually."

Munch sighed, reluctantly putting the pie back. "Fine, fine. But… one last bite?" he asked, looking hopeful.

Sammy couldn't help but laugh. "Alright, one last bite. But after that, you're done with midnight cafeteria runs. Deal?"

"Deal!" Munch grinned, happily taking one final, triumphant bite of pie.

The Final Farewell of the Phantom

The next morning, Sammy overheard one last rumour about the "Phantom of the Cafeteria." According to the latest tale, the phantom had "vanished into the night," leaving behind only a few mysterious crumbs and the faint memory of a cheerful hum.

With Munch's midnight escapades officially over, the campus buzz about the phantom began to fade. But for Sammy and his monster friends, the story of the "Phantom Diner" would remain a hilarious, unforgettable chapter in their college adventure.

Later that night, as Munch recounted his "legendary" status with pride, Sammy couldn't help but laugh. His friend might have retired as the phantom, but his appetite for adventure—and snacks—was far from over.

Chapter 18: The Campus Ghost Hunt

It was a chilly October evening, and the campus was buzzing with rumours of a ghost sighting. Students were whispering about eerie shadows, strange sounds, and even floating objects in the old administration building. Most dismissed it as just a story to spook new students, but the rumours grew louder each day, with everyone wondering if there was truly a ghost haunting the campus.

As Sammy returned to his dorm, he found his monster friends gathered, each one looking excited—especially Mumbles, whose eyes were practically glowing with anticipation.

"Sammy, we have to check this out!" Mumbles whispered, his voice barely more than a ghostly breeze. "A campus ghost? This is a chance to meet someone from my world!"

Whiffle bounced with excitement, glitter spilling from his fur. "Imagine! A real ghost friend. And think of all the ghostly tricks we could learn!"

Blinky nodded, his glow flickering like a lantern. "We'll need to investigate carefully. Who knows what kind of spirit we're dealing with?"

Munch was already munching on a handful of popcorn, grinning. "I'm in! If there's a ghost, I bet they'll need a snack!"

Sammy chuckled. "Alright, team. Let's go ghost hunting."

Setting Out on the Ghost Hunt

As night fell, Sammy and his friends made their way to the old administration building, the supposed center of the ghost sightings. The building loomed in the moonlight, its windows dark and mysterious. Shadows flickered across the walls, and the faint rustle of leaves added to the eerie atmosphere.

Mumbles floated forward, his voice a soft whisper. "Follow me—I know how to spot a spirit. I'll lead the way."

They crept through the front entrance, keeping as quiet as possible. Mumbles floated ahead, his usually shy demeanour replaced by a sense of purpose. He seemed in his element, his whispers growing softer, more careful.

As they explored, Blinky's glow provided a warm, steady light, casting long shadows on the walls. The building was filled with empty offices, old bookshelves, and dusty furniture. Sammy could feel his heart pounding, both from excitement and a hint of nervousness.

The First "Sighting"

They rounded a corner and entered a large room, filled with tall stacks of boxes and old filing cabinets. Just as they stepped inside, a sudden, chilling sound echoed through the room—a low, eerie moan.

Sammy's eyes widened, and he looked around, half-expecting to see a figure floating by. But when he glanced at his friends, he noticed Munch trying—and failing—to stifle a laugh, his cheeks stuffed with popcorn.

"Munch!" Sammy hissed. "Were you... pretending to be a ghost?"

Munch grinned sheepishly, bits of popcorn falling from his mouth. "I couldn't help it! The atmosphere got to me!"

Mumbles chuckled softly, floating up next to Munch. "Not bad, Munch. But if you want to sound like a real ghost, you have to do it like this." He let out a soft, bone-chilling moan that echoed around the room, making everyone—even Sammy—jump a little.

Munch gave him an approving nod. "Okay, now that's spooky."

Strange Shadows and Whispering Walls

As they moved further into the building, they noticed shadows shifting on the walls, flickering in and out of sight. Blinky's glow wavered slightly, casting strange shapes and figures along the corridors.

"This is the perfect place for a ghost to hide," Blinky whispered. "Look at all these shadows..."

Sammy watched as Whiffle's glitter mixed with Blinky's light, creating swirling patterns in the air. The combination made the shadows look almost alive, like ghostly figures dancing on the walls.

Just then, a soft, whispering sound drifted toward them. Sammy felt a chill run down his spine.

"Is that... is that you, Mumbles?" he asked, half-expecting it to be another trick.

But Mumbles shook his head. "No, Sammy. That wasn't me."

The group huddled closer together, glancing around the empty hall. The whispers seemed to be coming from the end of the hallway, luring them forward.

"Let's check it out," Sammy said, feeling both brave and a little nervous. They tiptoed down the hall, Mumbles leading the way.

The "Ghostly" Encounter

At the end of the hall, they found an old storage room. Inside, the shelves were lined with stacks of papers, old books, and forgotten equipment. Just as they stepped in, they heard a sudden clatter from the far corner of the room.

Sammy's heart skipped a beat. He turned slowly, half-expecting to see a ghostly figure standing there. But instead, he saw a shadowy figure moving among the shelves, faintly shimmering.

"Hello...?" Sammy called out, his voice trembling slightly.

The figure paused, then slowly turned to face them. To everyone's surprise, it was not a ghost at all, but the campus custodian, an older woman who had been cleaning up the forgotten rooms. She wore a headlamp, casting a faint, ghostly glow as she moved through the dusty shelves.

"Oh!" she said, startled by the sight of Sammy and his friends. "What are you kids doing here?"

Sammy quickly recovered from the surprise. "Uh... we thought we heard a ghost. There've been rumours around campus..."

The custodian chuckled, shaking her head. "A ghost, huh? Well, I suppose it's easy to mistake shadows and creaks for something spooky in a place like this. But trust me, I'm the only one haunting these halls at night."

Everyone laughed, feeling a mixture of relief and disappointment.

The Ghostly Plan

As they left the building, Mumbles sighed, a little disheartened. "I was really hoping to meet a fellow ghost."

Sammy patted him on the back. "Don't worry, Mumbles. Maybe there isn't a real ghost on campus, but that doesn't mean we can't have a little fun."

Blinky's glow brightened with excitement. "You mean... we could be the ghost?"

Sammy grinned, nodding. "Exactly. Let's give the campus a little thrill."

The Campus "Ghost" Appears

Over the next few nights, Sammy and his friends took turns creating ghostly pranks around campus. Mumbles led the way, letting out soft, eerie whispers that drifted through the hallways of the old buildings. Blinky's glow cast mysterious lights, flickering in windows and along empty corridors.

Whiffle left trails of glitter that sparkled faintly in the moonlight, adding a magical, unearthly touch to their ghostly appearances. Munch provided the "evidence" by scattering a few crumbs in strategic locations, leaving students wondering if the ghost was a snack-loving spirit.

The rumours of a campus ghost grew even louder, and students began sharing stories of mysterious lights, strange sounds, and even a glowing figure floating through the night.

A Final Spooky Surprise

On Halloween night, Sammy and his friends put on their biggest ghostly performance yet. They dressed Mumbles in a makeshift white sheet, adding Blinky's glow for an extra eerie effect. Whiffle sprinkled glitter around him, and Munch stood by, tossing popcorn that looked like ghostly "ectoplasm" in the dim light.

They waited until the campus courtyard was full of students heading to Halloween events, then let Mumbles drift slowly across the lawn, his glowing form flickering in and out of sight.

Students gasped, pointing and whispering. "It's the campus ghost!"

As Mumbles floated by, he let out a soft, chilling moan, and the students scattered, both thrilled and spooked.

After the grand performance, Mumbles, Blinky, Whiffle, Munch, and Sammy retreated to a quiet corner, laughing and congratulating each other on their success.

"That was the best ghost hunt ever," Whiffle said, still giggling.

"And maybe even better because we got to be the ghost," Mumbles added with a proud smile.

Sammy grinned, looking around at his friends. "I think we made this Halloween one to remember."

As they headed back to their dorm, the night filled with laughter and ghostly memories, Sammy knew he'd never forget their campus ghost hunt—and the night his friends became the legends of campus lore.

Chapter 19: The Dorm Room Dance Party

It was a Friday night, and Sammy's week had been packed with exams, papers, and endless study sessions. Now, all he wanted was a chance to unwind, let loose, and have a bit of fun with his friends. He was sprawled out on his bed, wondering what to do, when Blinky floated over, his glow bright and enthusiastic.

"Sammy," Blinky said with a grin, "I think it's time we throw a party. Not just any party—a monster-sized dance party."

Sammy sat up, his eyes lighting up with excitement. "You mean... right here? In the dorm?"

Blinky nodded, his glow pulsing to the beat of an imaginary rhythm. "I'll handle the lighting, Whiffle can add some sparkle, Munch can bring snacks, and Mumbles... well, he can keep things mysterious."

Sammy grinned, already imagining the possibilities. "Alright, Blinky. Let's turn this room into a mini-nightclub."

Transforming the Dorm Room

With Blinky leading the way, Sammy and his monster friends got to work. Blinky positioned himself in the corner of the room, dimming and brightening his glow to create an atmospheric, pulsing light. He experimented with different colors—deep blue, neon pink, and glowing green—turning the room into a rainbow of shifting lights.

Whiffle added his own touch, sprinkling glitter around the room so that each pulse of Blinky's light made the air shimmer. Every step Sammy took left a little trail of sparkles behind him, adding an extra magical touch to the space.

Mumbles floated around, whispering softly in his ghostly voice, creating a cool, mysterious vibe. Whenever his whispers drifted through the room, it felt like the walls themselves were humming along with the beat.

And of course, Munch took over snack duty, arranging a spread of popcorn, mini sandwiches, cookies, and a mountain of candy on Sammy's desk. "No dance party is complete without snacks," Munch declared, grabbing a handful of popcorn to munch on.

As they finished setting up, Sammy looked around, amazed. His dorm room had been transformed into a cozy, glowing nightclub, complete with mood lighting, shimmering sparkles, and an array of snacks.

The Music and the Moves

Blinky floated over to Sammy's phone and used his glow to tap it, starting up a playlist Sammy had been working on. The first song boomed through the speakers, filling the room with an upbeat rhythm that instantly had everyone moving.

Sammy let out a cheer and started dancing, throwing his hands in the air and tapping his feet to the beat. Blinky pulsed his light in sync with the music, flashing in time to the rhythm, making it feel like a real club.

Whiffle, unable to resist the beat, joined in with his own bouncy moves, spinning in circles and leaving a trail of glitter that sparkled in Blinky's light. "Look at me, Sammy!" Whiffle called, twirling so fast that he looked like a glittery tornado.

Munch, ever the snack enthusiast, danced his way over to the snack table, grooving as he grabbed handfuls of popcorn and candy to keep his energy up. He started doing a little "munch and groove" dance, popping a bite into his mouth with each move.

Even Mumbles, usually reserved and quiet, swayed along, his soft whispers blending with the music, creating an almost ethereal harmony. He floated through the room like a mist, his presence adding a mysterious element to the party.

Glow-In-The-Dark Dance-Off

Halfway through the playlist, Blinky dimmed the lights even further, making his glow stand out against the darkness. "Let's make this a glow-in-the-dark dance-off!" he announced, turning himself into a rotating disco ball.

Sammy laughed, throwing himself into the challenge. He and his friends each took turns showing off their moves, trying to outdo each other.

Sammy started with a few classic moves, throwing in some silly dance steps that had everyone laughing. He even attempted the "worm," making his friends cheer and clap.

Whiffle took his turn next, doing a series of spins, jumps, and glittery cartwheels that left sparkles in the air. Each twirl created a swirl of glitter that looked like stardust floating in the glow of Blinky's light.

Munch's dance moves were enthusiastic but snack-focused; he wiggled, spun, and grooved while holding a cookie in each hand. His "snack shimmy" became the highlight of the night, with Munch dancing and snacking simultaneously, never missing a beat.

Then, it was Mumbles' turn. True to his mysterious nature, he floated gracefully, his movements soft and flowing, almost like he was gliding through water. He created a ghostly, mesmerizing dance that left trails of invisible ink designs in the air, each one glowing faintly in Blinky's light.

Finally, Blinky turned his glow up to the max, his lights shifting colors rapidly. He spun around like a true disco ball, flashing different colors in time to the beat, creating an incredible light show that filled the entire room. Sammy and the monsters cheered, clapping and laughing as Blinky's lights pulsed with the energy of the music.

A Snack Break with Monster Games

After dancing for what felt like hours, Sammy and his friends took a break, gathering around the snack table. Munch had set up a mini "snack station," and everyone grabbed their favorite treats.

As they munched, Whiffle suggested they play a quick game of "Monster Freeze Dance." Each time Blinky stopped the music, they all had to freeze in place until it started again. The game quickly turned hilarious, with Munch freezing mid-bite, Sammy balancing on one foot, and Whiffle pausing mid-sparkle.

Whenever Mumbles froze, he would disappear from sight, leaving only his faint whispers floating in the air, adding a spooky touch to the game. And each time Blinky hit the play button again, the room erupted in laughter as they tried to get back into the groove.

The Ultimate Light Show Finale

As the night wore on, Sammy realized it was almost time to wrap up the party. But Blinky, ever the showman, had one last surprise in store.

"Alright, everyone! Gather around for the grand finale!" Blinky announced, his glow pulsing with excitement.

He dimmed his light to almost complete darkness, letting everyone's eyes adjust. Then, slowly, he began to increase his brightness, shifting from a faint glow to a radiant, multi-coloured light show. He spun around the room, casting beams of light in every direction, creating dancing shadows and bright bursts of color.

Whiffle added his final touch, throwing a handful of glitter into the air, which sparkled and shimmered in Blinky's light, like a thousand tiny stars twinkling around them.

The music reached its peak, and everyone joined in one last dance, laughing and cheering as they danced through the glitter-filled, glowing room. The energy was contagious, filling Sammy with pure joy and laughter as he danced with his friends, their carefree spirits making it a night to remember.

The Afterparty Glow

As the final song ended, everyone flopped onto the bed and floor, out of breath but grinning from ear to ear. Glitter covered nearly every surface, and the faint glow of Blinky's light cast a soft, warm glow over the room.

"That was the best dance party ever," Sammy said, still catching his breath. "Thanks, Blinky. And thanks to all of you."

Whiffle beamed. "Anytime, Sammy! We should do this every week!"

Munch, munching on his last cookie, nodded in agreement. "Agreed. Best party snacks ever."

Mumbles gave a quiet nod, his smile soft. "We brought a little magic to the night, didn't we?"

Sammy looked around at his friends, his heart swelling with gratitude. He knew he was incredibly lucky to have friends who could turn an ordinary dorm room into a place of joy, magic, and laughter.

As they all settled down, Blinky dimmed his glow to a soft, peaceful light, casting a calm, cozy ambiance over the room. They sat quietly, enjoying the moment, each one feeling content and happy.

And as Sammy drifted off to sleep that night, he knew that this was a memory he would treasure—a night of dancing, laughter, and pure monster magic.

Chapter 20: The Great Roommate Swap

It all began one evening when Sammy was venting to his monster friends about his roommate, Jake. Jake was a great guy, but they had some minor clashes over things like where to store snacks, who used the most desk space, and, of course, who left their things lying around the most.

"I mean, he's not doing it on purpose," Sammy said, "but it's like we're on different wavelengths with our stuff! I think we just have different habits."

Whiffle's eyes sparkled with mischief. "I think we can help with that. Why don't we give him a little... gentle reminder to think about things from your perspective?"

Blinky nodded, grinning. "And you can try seeing things from his side too. A little room swap could be exactly what you need to understand each other better."

Sammy raised an eyebrow, intrigued. "What do you have in mind?"

Whiffle smirked, tossing a bit of glitter in the air. "Let's say we make a few subtle changes in the room—a little switch here, a swap there—so you both get a taste of each other's habits. Nothing too big, but just enough to make things interesting!"

Sammy couldn't help but laugh. "Alright, let's do it! Let the great roommate swap begin."

The First Subtle Swap

They started small. While Jake was out studying, the monsters helped Sammy move a few of Jake's things to Sammy's side of the room. Whiffle and Mumbles swapped Jake's water bottle and laptop charger onto Sammy's desk, while Blinky moved Jake's books to Sammy's shelves, leaving everything in the same spot but just enough out of place.

When Jake returned later that evening, he paused, looking around in confusion. "Hey, Sammy... why is my charger on your desk?"

Sammy shrugged, pretending to be just as puzzled. "I have no idea! Maybe we got our stuff mixed up?"

Jake scratched his head. "Weird. Guess we should pay more attention to where we put things."

Sammy and his friends exchanged sneaky grins. Step one of the swap was a success.

The Snack Shuffle

The next day, Munch took charge of the snack situation. Knowing that Sammy and Jake had different tastes—Sammy preferred healthy snacks like nuts and fruit, while Jake was all about chips and candy—Munch had the idea to swap their snack stashes.

After Jake left for class, Munch took all of Sammy's nuts and granola bars and placed them in Jake's snack drawer. Then, he filled Sammy's snack bin with Jake's candy and chips.

When Jake came back later and went to grab a snack, he looked at Sammy's snack bin with confusion. "Sammy, did you get into my snacks?"

Sammy laughed, shrugging innocently. "Nope, that's all yours!"

Jake held up a handful of almonds, grinning. "Well, I guess I'm trying something new today." They both laughed, but Sammy could tell that the swap had made Jake think a little about their different tastes.

The Clothing Conundrum

Next, Whiffle decided to add a touch of personal style to the mix. Sammy and Jake each had their own designated spots for their coats and shoes—Sammy's neatly lined up, Jake's in a pile near his bed. So, Whiffle switched a few of their items around.

Jake's favorite hoodie was draped over Sammy's chair, and Sammy's shoes were placed near Jake's bed. Whiffle even swapped their hats, leaving Jake's on Sammy's shelf and Sammy's on Jake's.

When Jake noticed, he scratched his head in bewilderment. "Okay, either I'm losing my mind, or my stuff keeps moving around on its own."

Sammy pretended to be just as confused. "Maybe the dorm has a poltergeist?"

Jake laughed, but Sammy could see him thinking about it. He looked at his pile of clothes, then at Sammy's organized side, as if realizing the difference in their habits.

Study Supplies Surprise

For the next swap, Blinky took charge. He noticed that Jake tended to spread his study supplies all over his desk, while Sammy kept his things in neat piles. To give Jake a taste of Sammy's style, Blinky spent a few minutes rearranging Jake's desk, putting his notebooks, pens, and laptop in tidy, organized stacks.

When Jake returned and saw his newly organized desk, he looked around in surprise. "Sammy... did you organize my stuff?"

Sammy shrugged with a smile. "Guess it's a new look. How does it feel?"

Jake chuckled, sitting down at his now-organized desk. "Actually... it feels kind of nice." He reached for a pen, his eyes scanning the neatly arranged space with newfound appreciation. "Maybe I'll try to keep it this way."

Sammy grinned, realizing the subtle swap was working better than he'd expected.

The Final Touch: A Note Exchange

Mumbles added the finishing touch to their swap plan by sneaking in a few notes between Sammy and Jake's belongings. Each note had a small message, reminding them to see things from each other's perspective.

Jake found a note tucked under his laptop that read: "Try seeing things from a different angle." Later, Sammy discovered a similar note in his textbook, saying: "A little change in perspective can go a long way."

Each time they found a new note, they laughed, exchanging glances that showed they were both starting to understand the point of the swaps.

A Newfound Appreciation

By the end of the week, Sammy and Jake had gone through a whirlwind of little swaps. Jake had tried some of Sammy's healthier snacks, organized his desk, and even kept his shoes neatly lined up for once. Meanwhile, Sammy found himself loosening up a bit, leaving his water bottle or pen lying around every now and then.

On Friday evening, as they sat on their beds, Jake laughed, shaking his head. "I don't know if it's just me, but this week has felt... different. It's like our stuff has been swapping sides all week."

Sammy chuckled, deciding it was time to fess up. "Jake... it was a little experiment. My friends and I thought it'd be fun to see what it'd be like if we each tried living with each other's habits for a bit."

Jake laughed, nodding. "So that's what this was about! I should've guessed." He thought for a moment, then smiled. "Actually, I think it was a good idea. I kind of liked having a neater desk, and... your snacks aren't half-bad."

Sammy grinned. "And hey, I'm starting to appreciate a little mess every now and then. Makes things feel more relaxed."

Roommate Harmony

By the end of their "swap week," Sammy and Jake had come to understand each other a little better. They laughed about their habits, appreciated each other's quirks, and even made a few small changes to accommodate each other. Jake kept his desk a bit tidier, while Sammy loosened up about having a perfectly organized side of the room.

That night, as Sammy told his monster friends about their successful plan, they all cheered.

"Mission 'Roommate Swap' complete!" Whiffle declared, throwing a handful of glitter into the air.

Munch raised a celebratory cookie. "Here's to a job well done and snacks well-shared."

Mumbles gave a soft, satisfied smile. "Sometimes, all it takes is a little nudge in the right direction."

Blinky pulsed his glow with pride. "And a bit of light to help see things from the other side."

As they celebrated, Sammy felt grateful for his friends' creativity and teamwork. Thanks to them, he and Jake had found a new harmony in their shared space, proving that even the smallest swaps could lead to understanding—and a much happier dorm room.

Chapter 21: Finals Week Frenzy

It was finals week, and the stress in Sammy's dorm room was palpable. His desk was piled high with books, notes, and practice tests, and the weight of the last big exam loomed over him like a dark cloud. Sammy's monsters watched him, their faces full of concern as he buried his head in a mountain of biology flashcards.

Munch was the first to speak up, nibbling on a cracker with a worried frown. "Sammy, you've been staring at those notes for hours. You need a break!"

Blinky nodded, his glow dimming slightly. "Finals can be rough, but you won't do your best if you're totally burnt out. I think it's time for a little monster-style study break."

Sammy looked up, exhausted but intrigued. "A study break? What do you have in mind?"

Whiffle grinned, tossing glitter in the air. "Leave it to us! By the end of the night, you'll be more relaxed, focused, and ready to crush that last final."

Sammy smiled, knowing he was in for an adventure. "Alright, I'm all yours. Let the finals week frenzy begin."

Monster-Style Study Breaks

The first study break took place right there at Sammy's desk. Blinky hovered over his pile of notes, illuminating each page with a calming, warm glow. "Here's the deal, Sammy," he said. "For every five flashcards you get right, you get a reward. And trust me, we've got some good ones lined up."

With a renewed sense of motivation, Sammy quizzed himself on the flashcards, calling out answers as he went. Each time he answered five correctly, Blinky rewarded him with a mini "glow show," sending sparkles of coloured light across his desk in fun patterns.

Whiffle added his own twist by tossing a sprinkle of glitter every time Sammy got a tough question right. Soon, Sammy's desk looked like a magical study zone, covered in shimmering sparkles and bathed in Blinky's colorful glow.

The Silly Dance Party Break

After Sammy had made it through a solid chunk of his notes, Munch called for a quick snack-and-dance break. He placed a bowl of popcorn in the middle of the room, cranked up Sammy's playlist, and started grooving to the beat.

"Dance it out, Sammy!" Munch called, shimmying in place with a handful of popcorn. "Moving around will wake you up and shake off the stress!"

Sammy laughed, unable to resist the infectious energy. He jumped up, dancing along with Munch as they threw silly moves into the mix. Whiffle twirled around them, his glitter swirling in the air like a miniature disco ball, while Blinky flashed his lights to match the rhythm of the music.

Even Mumbles joined in, floating gently along to the beat, his ghostly movements adding a spooky-fun vibe to their dance party. Sammy couldn't stop laughing as they all grooved together, his stress melting away with each step.

The Guided "Monster Meditation"

Once they'd danced out their energy, Mumbles suggested a calming activity to help Sammy reset his focus. "Let's do a quick meditation," Mumbles said softly. "A monster-style one, of course."

He dimmed the room's lights, leaving only Blinky's soft glow to cast a gentle warmth over them. Sammy closed his eyes, following Mumbles' soothing instructions.

"Imagine yourself floating through a peaceful, glittery cloud," Mumbles whispered, his voice calm and airy. "Each breath brings you a sense of calm. And with each exhale, you're letting go of stress."

As Mumbles spoke, Whiffle added a soft sprinkle of glitter that drifted down like tiny stars, making Sammy feel like he was floating in a magical sky. The calming effect was instant, and Sammy found himself relaxing, his thoughts clearing with each breath.

"Now," Mumbles continued, "picture yourself finishing your last final with confidence, knowing you've done your best."

Sammy took a deep breath, letting the comforting words sink in. When he opened his eyes, he felt refreshed, a little lighter, and ready to tackle more studying.

Snack Station "Refuel"

With Sammy feeling more energized, Munch set up a "refuel station" on his desk, complete with healthy snacks and a few treats for motivation.

"Alright, Sammy," Munch said, arranging a spread of apples, granola bars, and chocolate. "The deal is, every time you finish a chapter review, you get to pick a snack. Keeps the brain fuelled and ready!"

Sammy grinned, appreciating the encouragement. He returned to his studies, more focused than before, knowing that a tasty reward awaited him at each break.

As he completed each chapter, he enjoyed the snacks, laughing as Munch cheered him on with a mini dance every time he took a bite. Between the snacks and Munch's enthusiasm, Sammy felt more motivated than ever.

The Laughter Challenge

Finally, Whiffle decided it was time to shake things up with a laughter challenge. He sat across from Sammy, making goofy faces and telling silly jokes in an attempt to make him laugh.

"Why did the monster cross the road?" Whiffle asked, struggling to keep a straight face.

"Why?" Sammy asked, already smiling.

"To get to the other scream!" Whiffle said, bursting into laughter.

Sammy couldn't help it—he cracked up, laughing along with his friend. Each joke was funnier than the last, and soon everyone was joining in, adding their own puns and jokes to the mix. Even Mumbles let out a soft, ghostly chuckle, and Blinky's glow flickered with amusement.

The laughter filled the room, pushing away every last bit of Sammy's stress. By the end of it, his stomach hurt from laughing, but his mind felt clear and refreshed.

The Confidence Boost

As the night went on, Sammy completed his final review and set down his last stack of notes. He felt a little nervous, but also more prepared than he had all week.

Blinky floated over, giving him an encouraging smile. "Sammy, you've worked so hard. You know this material inside and out. We're all so proud of you."

Munch handed him a final snack—his favorite chocolate bar, saved just for this moment. "You're going to crush that final. Just remember to take deep breaths and trust yourself."

Whiffle added a sprinkle of glitter, giving Sammy's desk a little extra sparkle. "You're ready, Sammy. And no matter what, we'll be here to celebrate when you're done!"

Mumbles gave him a quiet nod, his smile reassuring. "You've got this, Sammy. Finals are no match for you."

Sammy's heart swelled with gratitude for his friends. He knew he'd been stressed out of his mind at the start of the week, but thanks to their support, he was heading into his last final feeling calm, prepared, and confident.

The Big Day

The next morning, Sammy walked into the exam room with a calm smile, remembering every joke, every snack, and every glow-filled study break his friends had given him. As he tackled each question, he could almost hear Blinky's encouragement, see Whiffle's glitter, and feel Mumbles' calming whispers reminding him to stay focused.

When he finished the test, he felt a huge sense of relief and accomplishment. He'd done it.

Celebrating the End of Finals

That night, Sammy returned to his dorm room to find his friends waiting for him with an impromptu celebration. Blinky's glow filled the room with festive colors, Whiffle had decorated the space with extra glitter, and Munch had set up a spread of treats and drinks. Mumbles had even prepared a congratulatory message written in invisible ink on Sammy's desk, which read: "You did it, Sammy!"

They all cheered as Sammy walked in, and Sammy couldn't stop grinning. "Thank you, guys. I don't know what I would've done without you this week."

Whiffle hugged him, leaving a trail of glitter. "You did amazing, Sammy. We knew you could do it!"

Munch handed him a celebratory cookie. "You survived finals week and still have energy to celebrate. That's impressive!"

Blinky's glow pulsed with pride. "And now you get to relax. You've earned it."

As they celebrated together, Sammy realized how lucky he was to have such incredible friends by his side. They'd turned his finals week frenzy into a time of laughter, encouragement, and warmth, proving that even the toughest challenges were easier to handle with friends who cared.

And as they laughed and toasted to the end of finals, Sammy knew he'd remember this week—and the friends who made it unforgettable—for a long time to come.

Chapter 22: The Monster Mascot Mystery

It was the day before the biggest game of the season, and the whole campus was buzzing with excitement. The football team was set to play their biggest rival, and students had decked out the campus in the school colors, chanting and cheering at every chance.

But just as the celebrations were getting started, a rumour spread through the crowd: the mascot had gone missing. Sammy heard the news as he walked to class, catching snippets of worried conversations from students passing by.

"Did you hear? The mascot costume is gone!"

"Who would take it right before the game?"

"If we don't have our mascot, it'll be bad luck!"

Sammy felt a pang of worry. The mascot, a giant, fluffy bear named Bruin, was a cherished campus symbol, known for its wild antics and hilarious dance moves. Losing it right before the big game felt like a disaster.

That evening, as Sammy told his monster friends about the missing mascot, they exchanged excited, mischievous glances.

Whiffle's eyes sparkled with excitement. "Did someone say missing mascot? I think we know the perfect replacements."

Blinky's glow pulsed in agreement. "Imagine it, Sammy—a team of monster mascots filling in! We could bring something extra special to game day."

Munch grinned, already munching on popcorn he'd "borrowed" from the concession stand. "And we can snack along the way. Win-win!"

Mumbles gave a quiet nod, his soft voice carrying a touch of pride. "Let's make it a game day they'll never forget."

Sammy laughed, knowing his friends wouldn't be talked out of it. "Alright, let's do it! The Monster Mascot Team is officially in session."

Creating the Monster Mascot Team

The next morning, Sammy and his friends snuck into the football stadium, where preparations were underway. The cheerleaders were practicing routines, students were hanging up banners, and the smell of popcorn and hot dogs filled the air.

With the mascot suit still missing, Whiffle, Blinky, Munch, and Mumbles took their positions as the official substitute mascots. They each added their own twist to their "uniforms": Whiffle wrapped himself in blue and gold streamers, Blinky created a glowing aura of school colors, Munch tied a giant foam finger to his head, and Mumbles floated through the air like a ghostly cheerleader, trailing wisps of school-coloured mist.

Sammy grinned at his friends' creative costumes. "You guys look amazing! The crowd's going to love it."

The monsters lined up at the stadium entrance, ready to make their debut. As the announcer introduced the team, Sammy stepped forward to explain the situation.

"Since our mascot has gone missing," he announced, "we've brought in some substitute mascots to keep the spirit alive!"

With that, the monsters bounded onto the field, greeted by cheers, laughter, and a few gasps of surprise.

Whiffle's Glittery Dance-Off

Whiffle started things off by leading a cheer, his blue and gold streamers swirling in every direction as he bounced around with boundless energy. He added his own touch by sprinkling glitter on the crowd as he danced along the sidelines, waving at the students and doing cartwheels with infectious enthusiasm.

The crowd loved him, chanting along as Whiffle led them in cheers, each one louder than the last. He even started a mini "dance-off" with a few brave students, spinning and twirling, leaving trails of glitter that sparkled in the sunlight.

"Whiffle! Whiffle!" the crowd chanted, totally enthralled by the glittery, cheerful substitute mascot.

Blinky's Glowing Halftime Show

When halftime rolled around, Blinky took center stage, transforming the field into a glowing spectacle. He dimmed the stadium lights and began pulsing his glow in time with the music, casting waves of blue and gold light across the stands.

He created glowing shapes that floated in the air—a paw print here, a starburst there—lighting up the stadium in a mesmerizing display. The crowd was mesmerized, waving glow sticks and flashlights to match Blinky's glowing patterns.

As the final song played, Blinky created a huge, glowing image of the missing mascot, Bruin the bear, as a tribute, sending the crowd into a cheering frenzy.

"Blinky! Blinky!" they chanted, awestruck by the unforgettable light show.

Munch's Snack Giveaway Frenzy

Never one to miss out on a snack opportunity, Munch took his place near the concession stands. With his foam finger and an armful of snacks, he went around the stands, tossing popcorn, candy, and small bags of chips to cheering fans.

"Get your game day snacks!" he yelled, tossing treats into the air like confetti. "Nothing better than free food!"

The students laughed, reaching out to catch the snacks, grateful for the unexpected treats. Munch even managed to lead a chant of "Snacks! Snacks! Snacks!" that echoed through the stadium, adding a touch of humour to the day.

Sammy watched from the sidelines, barely holding back laughter as he saw Munch bounce around, tossing snacks and dancing to the beat of the band.

Mumbles' Ghostly "Fan Waves"

As the game went on, Mumbles floated silently through the stands, adding a mysterious touch to the monster mascot team's antics. He would appear and disappear, hovering near groups of students and leading them in spooky "ghostly" cheers.

At one point, he led a "wave" through the stadium, appearing at the start of each section and moving along with his misty glow. Students screamed in excitement each time he passed, raising their arms in sync with his "ghostly" wave.

Mumbles even left a few cryptic messages on fans' programs, written in invisible ink that only revealed itself under the stadium lights, adding a playful touch of mystery to his mascot performance.

"Whoooo is the best team?" he whispered, his voice echoing eerily, making the students laugh and cheer.

The Big Finale

As the final quarter of the game approached, the monsters gathered in the middle of the field, each one ready to give the crowd a last unforgettable cheer. Sammy joined them, cheering as loud as he could, his heart full of pride for his friends' incredible performance.

Whiffle did one last glittery spin, Blinky sent beams of light dancing across the crowd, Munch tossed the last of his snacks, and Mumbles floated in eerie circles, creating a ghostly mist that enveloped the team.

As the final whistle blew, signalling the end of the game, the crowd roared in appreciation, chanting "Monsters! Monsters!" as a tribute to the team that had stepped in to keep the spirit alive.

A New Campus Legend

By the end of the night, Sammy and his friends were exhausted but thrilled. They'd saved game day and created a memory that would be talked about for years to come.

As they walked back to the dorms, still glowing from the excitement of the game, Whiffle tossed a bit of glitter into the air, his eyes sparkling with pride. "We did it, Sammy! We were the best mascot team ever!"

Blinky nodded, his glow flickering with satisfaction. "I think we might have started a new tradition. Who needs a regular mascot when you have a monster mascot team?"

Munch grinned, munching on a celebratory candy bar. "And the snacks weren't half-bad either!"

Mumbles floated alongside them, his smile soft. "It's not every day we get to be legends."

As they returned to the dorm, Sammy felt a deep sense of gratitude for his friends. They'd not only brought the spirit back to game day but had also created a memory that he and the entire campus would treasure forever.

And as he drifted off to sleep that night, Sammy couldn't help but think about the legacy they'd created: the monster mascot team, heroes of the field, and the spirit of game day.

Chapter 23: The Graduation Time Capsule

It was the last week of Sammy's first year, and campus was buzzing with end-of-year activities. While walking back to his dorm, he noticed a small group of students huddled around a spot in the campus gardens. Curious, he joined them and saw a metal box, rusted and old, being lifted out of the ground.

The students around him murmured excitedly, and one of them explained, "It's a time capsule! They buried this here fifty years ago!"

Sammy's eyes widened in wonder as he watched the students open the box. Inside were faded photos, handwritten notes, and small tokens from the past—a ticket stub from a concert, a worn-out pennant, and even a tiny stuffed bear, the old version of the campus mascot. Each item was a piece of history, capturing a moment in time for future generations.

As he returned to his dorm, Sammy told his monster friends about the discovery, and their reactions were immediate.

"We should make our own time capsule!" Whiffle exclaimed, his eyes sparkling with excitement. "Imagine! Future students could find our treasures one day."

Munch grinned, already nibbling on a cookie. "And we'll leave a few snacks too—never know when they'll need a little treat."

Blinky's glow brightened with anticipation. "Let's fill it with memories of all our adventures. It'll be our way of staying connected to this place, even after we're gone."

Sammy felt a rush of excitement. "Alright, let's do it. We'll make a time capsule and leave a little monster magic for the future."

Choosing the Perfect Items

Back in the dorm room, Sammy and his friends started gathering items for the time capsule. Each monster wanted to include something special, something that would represent all the magical, funny, and heartwarming moments they'd shared.

Whiffle's Glitter Jar:

Whiffle decided to fill a small jar with his signature glitter. "This is a bit of me," he explained, smiling. "Whenever anyone opens it, they'll feel a burst of happiness." He gave the jar a good shake, watching as the glitter swirled inside, a kaleidoscope of color and sparkle. He added a tiny note: "May your days be filled with glitter and joy!"

Blinky's Glow Stone:

Blinky selected a smooth, round stone and infused it with a gentle glow. "This stone has a bit of my light in it," he said, placing it carefully in the capsule. "Whenever the person finds this, it'll remind them that there's always light, even in the darkest times." Sammy smiled, feeling a sense of peace just looking at Blinky's stone.

Munch's Cookie Recipe:

Munch, predictably, wanted to share his love for snacks. He wrote out his favorite cookie recipe on a scrap of paper, decorating it with tiny doodles of cookies and cakes. "A snack recipe is a must," he said proudly. "Future students need to know the secret to great study snacks." To top it off, he placed a sealed cookie in the capsule, just in case the future students wanted a taste right away.

Mumbles' Invisible Ink Message:

Mumbles, always the mysterious one, wrote a short message in invisible ink on a small slip of paper. He wouldn't tell anyone what it said, just that it would reveal itself to the right person. "Sometimes, the best messages are the ones that can't be seen until the right moment," he whispered, tucking the note into the capsule. Sammy shivered with anticipation, knowing Mumbles' message would be something special.

Sammy's Contribution

Finally, it was Sammy's turn. He thought about all the adventures, the laughter, the challenges, and the quiet moments with his friends. He wanted to capture the essence of their time together.

He decided to write a letter to whoever would find the capsule. In the letter, he described each of his monster friends and the adventures they'd had. He shared stories of their pranks, their study breaks, and even the time they'd filled in as the campus mascot. Each story was a piece of his heart, and as he wrote, he felt a deep sense of gratitude for the memories they'd made.

At the bottom of the letter, he added a simple message: "Wherever you are, remember that magic is real, and friends make it stronger."

Sealing the Capsule

When each item was in place, they sealed the box with a small, enchanted lock Blinky had created. It glowed faintly, and Blinky explained, "This lock will only open when someone who truly believes in magic tries to open it."

They all agreed it was the perfect finishing touch.

Burying the Capsule

Late that night, they snuck out to a quiet, hidden spot on campus, a small patch under a large oak tree near the dorms. It was a place they often went to relax and stargaze, a place that felt like their own special corner of the campus.

Together, they dug a small hole, placing the capsule carefully inside. Each one said a few words, wishing for the future students to experience the same magic, friendship, and joy that they had.

Whiffle tossed a bit of glitter into the hole, Munch left a few cookie crumbs as "good luck," Blinky added a final glow to the ground, and Mumbles let out a soft, reassuring whisper that echoed through the trees.

When they finished, they covered the capsule with soil, patting it down and marking it with a small stone.

A Moment to Reflect

They sat together in a circle under the tree, enjoying the stillness of the night and the shared feeling of having left something meaningful behind.

Sammy looked at his friends, his heart full of gratitude. "You know, years from now, someone will find that capsule and discover all the memories we made together. It'll be like we're still here, a part of this campus."

Blinky's glow softened as he placed a comforting hand on Sammy's shoulder. "That's the beauty of memories. They stay with you, even when you've moved on."

Munch passed around a few leftover cookies, grinning. "Here's to the future—and to the snacks they'll make with my recipe."

Mumbles gave a soft, quiet smile. "And to the magic that lives on, even when we're not around to see it."

Whiffle sprinkled one last handful of glitter in the air, watching as it drifted and settled on the ground. "May whoever finds it have the best, most glitter-filled adventures."

They all sat quietly, soaking in the moment, feeling a sense of connection to the campus and to each other that was deeper than words.

A Legacy of Magic

As they walked back to the dorm, Sammy glanced back at the tree, imagining future students finding the capsule and discovering the magical items they'd left behind. He could picture their smiles, their wonder, and the spark of magic that would ignite in their hearts.

Sammy knew that no matter where life took him, this campus—and the memories they'd made—would always be a part of him. And now, thanks to their time capsule, a piece of that magic would stay with the campus, waiting for the right person to find it.

And as they returned to the dorm, laughing and reminiscing, Sammy felt an overwhelming sense of peace. They'd left their legacy, and the magic of their friendship would live on, sealed in memories for generations to come.

Chapter 24: The Return of the Glitter Bomb

It was Sammy's last week on campus, and emotions were running high. The end of an incredible year was just around the corner, and he couldn't help but feel a bittersweet mixture of excitement for summer and sadness about leaving the friends—and the magic—that had made his first year unforgettable.

One evening, while packing up his dorm room, Sammy felt a familiar, glittery tingle in the air. A soft, high-pitched giggle echoed from the hallway, and before he knew it, a glittery poof filled the room, leaving sparkles floating down like confetti.

"Sammy!" a cheerful voice squealed, and out of the glitter emerged none other than Glimmerpuff, the tiny, mischievous fairy-like creature who was known for her glitter-bomb entrances and exits. She looked as vibrant as ever, her tiny wings shimmering in every color of the rainbow, and her hair an explosion of sparkles.

"Glimmerpuff!" Sammy gasped, a grin spreading across his face. "I didn't think I'd see you again!"

Glimmerpuff twirled in mid-air, leaving a swirling trail of glitter behind her. "I wouldn't miss your final week on campus for anything! I'm here to make sure you go out with a bang. Or better yet, a glitter bomb!"

Just then, Whiffle, Blinky, Munch, and Mumbles appeared, their faces lighting up at the sight of their old friend.

"Glimmerpuff!" Whiffle shouted, bouncing up and down. "You're back! This calls for an all-out glitter fest!"

Glimmerpuff winked, her mischievous smile growing. "Then let's make Sammy's last week a memory filled with sparkle, laughter, and a bit of mayhem."

Operation: Glitter Trail

Glimmerpuff wasted no time getting started. Her first mission was "Operation: Glitter Trail." She flew through the dorm hallways, sprinkling colorful glitter over every door handle, window ledge, and stairway. Students wandering by noticed the sparkles with delight and amusement, each one leaving a little trail of glitter as they went.

Whiffle and Glimmerpuff teamed up to sneak into Sammy's classes, where they sprinkled a subtle dusting of glitter on each chair. Every time a student sat down, they'd stand up with a glittery surprise, spreading the sparkles everywhere they went.

Soon enough, the entire campus was covered in glitter trails, each one leading back to Sammy's dorm room, as if Glimmerpuff had left a sparkly map for people to follow. The students laughed, taking selfies with the glitter-covered benches, tables, and doorways, enjoying the unexpected burst of color and whimsy.

The Surprise Glitter Fountain

Glimmerpuff's next idea was her biggest yet. She enlisted Blinky's help to create a magical glitter fountain in the center of campus. They gathered near the main fountain late at night, Blinky glowing with excitement as Glimmerpuff prepared her ultimate glitter bomb.

With a few magical words, Glimmerpuff sprinkled her glitter dust over the water. Blinky added a soft, pulsing glow, and suddenly, the fountain erupted in colorful, sparkling water that glittered in the moonlight. Each drop shimmered with rainbow hues, cascading in sparkles and sending glittery mist into the air.

By morning, students gathered around the fountain, amazed at the unexpected, sparkly transformation. They reached out, catching the glittery water, and laughed as they found themselves covered in tiny, shimmering stars.

Sammy watched from a distance, grinning with pride. "You really outdid yourself, Glimmerpuff."

Glimmerpuff giggled, giving him a sly wink. "Oh, we're just getting started, Sammy."

Glittery Pranks and Laughter

The next day, Glimmerpuff continued her mission of mischief. With Munch's help, she set up small glitter bombs in some of the more popular campus hangout spots. The library? Glitter bombed. The student lounge? Covered in a thin layer of sparkly dust. Even the campus café had glittery accents decorating every table.

Each time a glitter bomb went off, students burst out laughing, some even clapping and cheering as glitter filled the air. They'd seen glitter pranks on campus before, but none quite like this. People began calling it "The Great Glitter Attack," and rumours spread about the mysterious "glitter fairy" who was bringing sparkle to every corner of campus.

Sammy laughed as he watched Glimmerpuff's antics, feeling grateful for the laughter she was bringing to everyone's final days on campus.

A Glittery Goodbye Gift

As Sammy's final day approached, Glimmerpuff decided it was time for a parting gift—a glittery keepsake for Sammy to remember his magical friends by. She gathered the rest of the monsters and explained her idea: a tiny jar filled with memories.

Each monster took a turn filling the jar with something special. Whiffle sprinkled his signature blue glitter inside, adding a note that read, "May your life be as bright and sparkly as you are."

Blinky added a small glowstone that pulsed with his light, nestled in the bottom of the jar. "A little light to guide you," he said softly, smiling at Sammy.

Munch included a tiny recipe scroll with his favorite cookie recipe, chuckling as he added, "Never forget the power of a snack."

Mumbles, as always, left a mysterious, invisible ink message on a slip of paper that only Sammy would be able to read under the right light. "For when you need a friend's voice in the quiet moments," Mumbles whispered, slipping the note into the jar.

Finally, Glimmerpuff sprinkled in her multi-coloured glitter and sealed the jar with a sparkling bow. "This is your reminder, Sammy," she said with a smile, "that you'll always carry a piece of our magic with you."

The Last Glitter Bomb

On Sammy's last night in the dorms, Glimmerpuff prepared one final, epic glitter bomb to send him off in style. She hovered near the doorway as he packed his last box, a mischievous smile on her face.

"Ready for one last surprise?" she asked, her voice brimming with excitement.

Sammy laughed, bracing himself. "Alright, Glimmerpuff. Hit me with your best shot."

With a delighted giggle, Glimmerpuff spun in the air, releasing a massive swirl of glitter that filled the entire room. Gold, blue, pink, green—all the colors burst into the air, sparkling and swirling like a mini firework show, casting shimmering lights across every surface.

Sammy stood in awe, laughing as the glitter drifted down, coating him and his belongings in sparkles. The room looked like a dreamscape, a memory made of light and color, a perfect farewell to the place that had been his home.

As the glitter settled, Sammy looked at Glimmerpuff and his monster friends, feeling a pang of sadness mixed with joy. "Thank you, all of you," he said, his voice full of emotion. "I don't think I could've made it through this year without you."

Whiffle hugged him, leaving a trail of glitter on his shoulder. "We're always with you, Sammy, whether you see us or not."

Blinky glowed warmly. "You've got our light, Sammy. Whenever you need it, just remember us."

Munch handed him a final cookie, grinning. "And don't forget the snacks!"

Mumbles gave him a gentle nod, whispering, "Wherever you go, we'll be there."

A Sparkling Farewell

As Sammy left his dorm room for the last time, he looked back, seeing the faint shimmer of glitter left behind, a final reminder of the magical year he'd shared with his friends. He carried the memory jar in his bag, feeling a quiet comfort knowing he'd always have a piece of them with him.

And as he walked across campus one last time, he noticed glitter trails everywhere, sparkling in the morning light—Glimmerpuff's parting gift, a trail of magic for him to follow.

Sammy couldn't help but smile as he imagined future students discovering the glitter trails and wondering about the mysterious "glitter fairy" who had brought so much joy to the campus. He knew that wherever he went, he'd carry the spirit of his monster friends with him, a reminder of the magic, laughter, and friendship that had changed his life.

And as he walked forward, leaving his first year behind, Sammy felt ready for whatever came next, knowing that his friends—and a little bit of magic—would always be by his side.

Chapter 25: Secret Room Under the Library

It was Sammy's last day on campus, and he was feeling a mix of excitement and nostalgia. He'd spent the day saying goodbye to his friends, professors, and favorite places, but there was one spot he hadn't yet visited: the library, his favorite place to study, read, and occasionally doze off in a cozy corner.

As he stepped into the library, his friends appeared one by one, each eager to spend a little more time together before Sammy left.

"Last day, huh?" Whiffle said, twirling in a small puff of glitter. "Think we can squeeze in one more adventure?"

Sammy chuckled, running a hand through his hair. "Honestly, I'd love one. This place is packed with secrets—there's bound to be something we haven't discovered."

Blinky's glow flickered with excitement. "Then let's explore. I heard some students mention a 'hidden room' that no one has ever found. Maybe today's the day!"

Munch was already rummaging through the snack bag he'd brought along. "A mystery under the library? Count me in. I brought provisions for the journey!"

Mumbles floated silently, his smile soft yet mysterious. "Some secrets are meant to be found... especially today."

Sammy felt a spark of curiosity ignite. His friends' excitement was contagious, and he knew this last adventure would be one he'd remember forever.

The Search for the Secret Room

They began by exploring the quiet corners of the library. They searched through dusty archives, ran their fingers along the shelves of old books, and even tapped on the walls, listening for hollow spots that might lead to something hidden.

After nearly an hour of searching, Whiffle's sharp eyes caught something strange—a slightly crooked bookshelf in the far corner of the basement level, half-hidden behind a dusty curtain. He pointed it out, bouncing with excitement.

"Look! This shelf isn't straight, and the books are all old journals. It has to be hiding something!"

They gathered around, studying the shelf closely. Blinky leaned in, his glow casting a faint light on the old, dusty books. He noticed a particular book with a strange symbol—a small, faded sun and moon intertwined. Without hesitation, he reached out and gave the book a gentle tug.

The book didn't budge, but instead, the entire shelf slowly swung open, revealing a narrow stone staircase descending into the darkness below.

Sammy's heart raced with excitement. "This is it—the secret room! Let's go."

Entering the Underground Room

They carefully made their way down the stairs, with Blinky lighting the way. The stairs led to a massive, hidden room filled with shelves upon shelves of ancient books, artifacts, and mysterious objects. The air smelled of old parchment and a faint hint of lavender, as if the room had been sealed off for centuries.

Each shelf was packed with strange and magical items. There were weathered scrolls, glass bottles filled with shimmering liquids, ancient quills, and stones that glowed faintly in the darkness. It was like stepping into another world.

Whiffle gasped in awe, his eyes wide as he took in the shelves. "This place is amazing! It's like a treasure trove of forgotten magic."

Munch immediately grabbed a dusty leather-bound book labelled "Snacks of the Ancient World" and started flipping through the pages with a grin. "Look at this! People used to eat honey cakes for energy spells. I think I found my new favorite cookbook."

Blinky examined a glowing crystal, mesmerized by the way it pulsed like a heartbeat. "These items have their own kind of magic. It's as if they're alive, waiting for someone to discover their secrets."

Discovering Mysterious Artifacts

As they explored, each friend found something that resonated with them.

Whiffle found a small glass vial filled with enchanted glitter that changed colors depending on his mood. He carefully slipped it into his pocket. "For extra sparkle whenever I need it," he said, winking.

Blinky discovered a dusty mirror that, when he looked into it, reflected a version of himself glowing with vibrant colors he'd never seen before. "It's like it's showing me my true light," he whispered, touched.

Munch stumbled upon an ancient recipe book that contained charms for enhancing the taste of food. He chuckled, tucking it under his arm. "This is going to make my snacks legendary."

Mumbles drifted to a shadowy corner, where he found an old, weathered compass. The compass didn't point north but instead swirled toward places where magic was strong. "I think it's meant to lead us to magic," he whispered, tucking it into his cloak.

Sammy's Special Find

As Sammy wandered through the room, his gaze fell on an old wooden box covered in carvings of stars, moons, and swirling patterns. Intrigued, he opened it, finding a single, worn-out leather journal inside. The pages were filled with the handwritten notes of a student from decades ago, describing their own magical discoveries and the adventures they'd had on campus.

Flipping through the pages, Sammy felt an instant connection. The student had written about finding hidden rooms, making new friends, and experiencing the magic of college life. In the margins, there were sketches of strange creatures, symbols, and heartfelt notes about friendship.

One entry stood out to Sammy: "If you've found this journal, then you, too, have uncovered the magic hidden in this place. May it always be with you, wherever you go."

Sammy closed the journal, feeling a sense of peace wash over him. He tucked it into his bag, knowing it would be a treasured keepsake of this magical time in his life.

A Farewell to the Secret Room

After a while, they gathered near the stairs, ready to leave the secret room but feeling a mixture of excitement and nostalgia. They knew this room, and the secrets within it, would remain a part of them forever.

Whiffle tossed a handful of glitter into the air, watching it sparkle in the dim light. "Here's to the best year ever. May every student who finds this place have adventures like ours."

Blinky's glow softened. "This room is full of memories, and now it holds ours too."

Munch left a small snack on one of the shelves—a carefully wrapped cookie with a note that read: "For the next explorer, from a friend."

Mumbles held up the magical compass, giving it one last look. "Magic is a journey. This room is just one stop along the way."

The Last Adventure

As they climbed the stairs, each one took a moment to look back at the room, the shelves filled with secrets and the air tingling with enchantment. Sammy felt his heart swell with gratitude. This place, like his friends, had become a part of him, a memory he'd carry wherever he went.

Once they were back in the main library, Sammy pushed the bookshelf back into place, sealing the secret room once more. They left, feeling like they'd completed a final, perfect adventure—a tribute to all the magical moments they'd shared.

A Parting Gift

That evening, Sammy and his friends gathered one last time in his dorm room. They laughed, reminisced, and shared their favorite memories. As a final gift, each monster left Sammy with a small, meaningful token.

Whiffle left a pinch of his enchanted glitter in a tiny vial, "For whenever you need a bit of sparkle in your life."

Blinky gave him a small crystal that glowed faintly in the dark. "A reminder that there's always light, even in the toughest times."

Munch left a copy of his cookie recipe, saying, "Remember, snacks make every moment better."

Mumbles slipped Sammy the magical compass, whispering, "Let it guide you to places where magic lives."

Sammy felt a pang of bittersweet joy as he hugged each friend, knowing they'd always be a part of him.

Chapter 26: The Farewell Feast

It was the last night of Sammy's first year, and the air was filled with both excitement and a touch of sadness. Sammy's friends knew they wanted to make this night special, and Munch, of course, had the perfect idea.

"We're throwing you a farewell feast, Sammy!" Munch declared, bouncing with excitement. "It's going to be a monster-style banquet, with all your favorite snacks and a few surprises!"

Sammy's face lit up. "A feast sounds amazing! But... how are we going to pull it off in the dorm?"

Munch gave him a mischievous wink. "Leave that to us. We're going to turn the common room into the best farewell party this campus has ever seen!"

With that, his friends sprang into action, each one bringing their unique touch to make the farewell feast unforgettable.

Transforming the Common Room

First, they tackled the decorations. Whiffle darted around the common room, sprinkling enchanted glitter across every surface. The glitter transformed the room, covering it in shimmering blue and gold sparkles that caught the light in magical, mesmerizing ways.

Blinky set up a series of glowing orbs in every corner, creating a soft, inviting light that gave the room a warm, festive atmosphere. Each orb pulsed in sync with the gentle background music they had playing, adding a rhythmic glow that made the room feel alive.

Mumbles added an air of mystery to the setup. He cast a faint, misty glow over the tables, giving the snacks and drinks a magical shimmer. Every now and then, the mist would swirl gently, creating shapes that seemed to dance along with the music.

Meanwhile, Munch took charge of the snacks. He'd spent the entire day baking, mixing, and preparing a spread of his best treats. There were mountains of cookies, bowls of popcorn, trays of mini sandwiches, and stacks of fruit and cheese—all arranged in a grand display fit for a feast.

As the room came together, Sammy watched in awe, feeling a wave of gratitude wash over him. His friends had truly outdone themselves.

The Banquet Begins

Once everything was ready, Sammy's friends gathered around him, each one grinning with pride. Munch led him to the head of the table, where a plate piled high with snacks awaited him.

"Tonight, Sammy, you are the guest of honour," Munch announced, beaming with excitement. "This feast is a celebration of all our adventures, laughter, and the memories we've made. Eat as much as you want!"

Sammy laughed, grabbing a cookie and biting into it. "Thank you all so much. This is amazing."

Whiffle twirled with excitement. "It's only amazing because it's for you, Sammy! Now, let's eat!"

They all dug in, filling plates with snacks and toasting with sparkling punch Munch had made just for the occasion. The room echoed with laughter, stories, and the occasional burst of glitter as Whiffle added an extra sparkle whenever someone said something funny.

Magic and Memories

After they'd eaten their fill, Sammy's friends decided it was time to share a few memories.

Whiffle began, his eyes bright. "Remember that time we had the glittery burping contest? You almost beat me, Sammy! Almost."

Everyone laughed, remembering the hilarity of that impromptu contest, the glitter filling the air as they each tried to outdo one another.

Blinky added his memory next. "I'll never forget the midnight lab experiment we snuck into. Watching you discover glowing chemical reactions was a highlight of the year."

Sammy chuckled, feeling a warm glow at the memory. "I think we're lucky we didn't get caught!"

Mumbles' voice was soft and wistful as he shared his memory. "The campus ghost hunt. Seeing everyone look for the 'phantom' and hearing the laughter that followed—it was pure magic."

Munch was last. "Every snack we shared, every bite of popcorn, and every cookie. Those were the best moments. Because what's a party without a snack?"

Sammy's heart felt full as he listened to his friends, each memory a reminder of the incredible year they'd shared. He knew that he'd cherish these moments forever.

A Toast to Friendship

As the evening went on, Blinky called for a toast. He held up his glass, his glow bright and steady.

"To friendship," he said, his voice filled with warmth. "And to Sammy, for bringing us together and making every day brighter."

Everyone raised their glasses, echoing, "To friendship!" and "To Sammy!"

Sammy couldn't hide his smile, feeling both honoured and humbled. "Thank you, everyone. You've made this year more magical than I could have ever imagined."

Whiffle tossed a handful of glitter in the air, which settled gently over everyone, sparkling like stardust. "Here's to the magic of new adventures, wherever they take us."

A Farewell Gift

Just as the feast was winding down, Munch reached into his bag and pulled out a small box wrapped in shimmering paper. He handed it to Sammy with a grin.

"Open it!" he urged, his excitement contagious.

Sammy carefully unwrapped the box, revealing a small, leather-bound notebook with a sparkly, enchanted cover. Each friend had written a message on the first few pages, filling it with memories, wishes, and little doodles. The pages sparkled slightly, and as Sammy flipped through, he realized the notebook wasn't just any notebook—it had been enchanted to add new pages as he filled it, creating a never-ending journal.

Whiffle grinned. "Now you'll always have a place to write down new memories, even after you leave."

Blinky nodded. "And every time you write, you'll have a piece of us with you."

Munch chuckled. "Plus, there's a section just for snack ideas. Had to make sure of that."

Mumbles placed a hand on Sammy's shoulder. "This is just the beginning, Sammy. Wherever you go, remember that magic is everywhere—you just have to look."

Sammy's eyes grew misty as he hugged each of his friends, feeling the love and warmth radiating from them. This notebook was more than a gift; it was a symbol of everything they'd shared.

The Final Farewell

As the evening came to an end, Sammy and his friends lingered in the common room, reluctant to say goodbye. They laughed, shared more stories, and watched the glitter settle as the night grew quieter.

Finally, it was time to go. Sammy hugged each of his friends one last time, his heart brimming with gratitude.

"Thank you for everything," he said, his voice filled with emotion. "You've made this year unforgettable."

Whiffle, Blinky, Munch, and Mumbles smiled, each one giving him a final word of encouragement and a promise that they'd always be with him in spirit.

As they left the common room, Sammy looked back at the glitter-covered tables, the glowing lights, and the cozy warmth of the decorations. This was more than just a farewell feast—it was a memory, a celebration of friendship, and a reminder that no matter where he went, he'd always carry a bit of magic with him.

And as he walked back to his dorm, clutching the notebook and thinking of his friends, Sammy felt ready for whatever adventures lay ahead. The farewell feast was just the beginning of a lifetime filled with magic, laughter, and friendship.

Chapter 27: The Last Midnight Adventure

It was the final night on campus, and Sammy's bags were packed, ready for the journey home. But as he lay in bed, a familiar restlessness kept him awake. He knew there was one last adventure waiting to be had. His monster friends sensed it too, each one glancing at him with a twinkle in their eyes.

Blinky hovered by the window, his glow casting a gentle light over the room. "Sammy," he whispered, his voice filled with warmth and nostalgia, "are you up for one last adventure?"

Sammy sat up, grinning. "Absolutely. Let's go."

Whiffle clapped his hands in excitement, scattering glitter. "One last midnight journey across campus! Let's visit all our favorite spots!"

Munch grabbed his snack bag, stuffing it with treats. "I'm bringing snacks for the road. What's an adventure without fuel?"

Mumbles nodded, his smile soft and a little sad. "Tonight, we'll say goodbye the best way we know how—under the stars, with a touch of magic."

Together, they slipped out of the dorm room and into the cool, quiet night, ready for one last campus tour filled with memories, laughter, and a sprinkle of magic.

The Glittering Fountain

Their first stop was the fountain in the center of campus. Under the starlit sky, the fountain's water shimmered in Blinky's glow, creating soft, twinkling reflections.

Whiffle approached the edge of the fountain, his eyes bright. "This fountain has seen so much magic this year! It deserves a proper farewell."

He held his hands out, sending a gentle shower of glitter over the water. As the glitter settled, the fountain's water began to glow faintly, taking on a magical, shimmering quality.

Sammy laughed, dipping his fingers into the water and watching the glitter swirl around his hand. "Feels like we're leaving a little bit of ourselves here."

Munch pulled out a few cookies, handing one to each of them as they sat by the fountain. They munched quietly, watching the glittery water dance under the stars, savouring the calm and the magic of the moment.

The Library's Hidden Corner

Next, they made their way to the library, where so many late-night study sessions (and a few pranks) had taken place. The building was dark and silent, but the familiar smell of old books lingered in the air.

Blinky led them to their favorite hidden corner, a cozy nook where they'd spent hours laughing, studying, and sharing stories. He brightened his glow just enough to cast a soft, golden light, illuminating the dusty shelves and stacks of old books.

"Remember the secret room we found under the library?" Blinky said, his glow pulsing with excitement. "I don't think I'll ever forget that adventure."

Sammy ran his fingers along the spines of the books, each one holding memories of study breaks, whispered conversations, and moments of discovery. "This library... it was our little world, wasn't it?"

Mumbles left a faint mist that swirled through the air, giving the nook an ethereal glow. "Our memories will linger here, waiting for the next curious soul to find them."

The Great Lawn

Their next stop was the great lawn, where they had celebrated the big game and hosted the infamous monster mascot team. Tonight, it was empty and serene, bathed in moonlight, with only the soft rustling of leaves filling the air.

Whiffle did a playful twirl, tossing a sprinkle of glitter that settled over the grass like dewdrops. "This place saw so many of our antics! The dance parties, the ghostly waves during the big game... it's like we left pieces of our laughter here."

Sammy couldn't help but smile as he remembered those nights. "And who could forget the glitter fountain? You really outdid yourself, Whiffle."

They sat on the grass, looking up at the stars, each one lost in memories of all the fun they'd shared. Munch pulled out a bag of popcorn, and they munched quietly, each one basking in the magic of the night.

The Dorm Rooftop

Finally, they made their way to the rooftop of Sammy's dorm, their ultimate secret spot for stargazing and late-night talks. The campus stretched out below them, quiet and beautiful, with lights twinkling in the distance.

Blinky brightened, casting a gentle glow that felt like a warm embrace. "This rooftop... we've had some of our best talks here, haven't we?"

Sammy nodded, feeling a surge of gratitude. "Yeah, this place became home because of you guys. I don't think I would've made it through the year without you."

Whiffle tossed a sprinkle of glitter into the night air, watching it drift and sparkle like stardust. "You brought magic into our lives too, Sammy. You'll always be part of our world, no matter where you go."

Mumbles whispered softly, his voice blending with the night breeze. "The magic is in the memories we've made. Those memories will stay with you, even when we're apart."

They sat in silence, each one looking up at the stars, knowing this was their last night together on campus. The quiet was filled with a shared understanding, a bittersweet feeling of both endings and beginnings.

A Magical Goodbye

As dawn began to break, the sky lightened, casting a soft glow over the campus. Sammy and his friends stood together, watching as the first rays of sunlight touched their favorite places—the fountain, the library, the lawn, and finally the rooftop.

Blinky held out his hand, his glow flickering gently. "This isn't really goodbye, Sammy. You'll carry us with you, just like we'll carry you with us."

Munch passed Sammy a small bundle wrapped in cloth. Inside was a cookie, a pinch of glitter, and a tiny glowstone—tokens of their friendship, symbols of each monster's unique magic.

Whiffle wrapped Sammy in a hug, his glitter leaving a sparkling trail on Sammy's shoulder. "Whenever you need a little magic, remember us."

Mumbles hovered close, his voice barely a whisper. "Friendship is the truest magic, Sammy. No matter where you go, it's with you."

Sammy's heart felt full as he hugged each of them, feeling their warmth, their magic, and their love.

"Thank you, all of you," he said, his voice thick with emotion. "This year has been... everything. I'll never forget it."

With one last look around, they made their way down from the rooftop. As they walked back through the dorm, Sammy felt the weight of all the memories they'd made, each one a reminder of the magic of friendship, laughter, and shared adventures.

One Last Glittery Trail

As Sammy returned to his dorm room to grab his bags, Whiffle left a final trail of glitter leading from the door to the rooftop. It sparkled in the early morning light, a quiet reminder of the friends he'd leave behind but never forget.

He knew that wherever life took him, he'd carry the spirit of his monster friends with him. They'd taught him that magic existed not just in glitter, glows, and ghostly whispers, but in the bonds they'd formed and the memories they'd created together.

As Sammy left campus, he glanced back one last time, feeling a sense of peace. His first year had come to an end, but thanks to his friends, he'd learned that every ending held the promise of new beginnings.

And with their magic and love woven into his heart, Sammy stepped forward, ready for the next adventure, wherever it might lead.

Chapter 28: The Letter of Monster Memories

The morning was quiet as Sammy sat at his desk for one final time. His bags were packed, the room was bare, and campus stretched out in the early light, waiting to say goodbye. But before he left, there was one last thing he needed to do. He pulled out a notebook and a pen, and took a deep breath, preparing to put into words everything he felt.

With a warm smile and a heart full of gratitude, he began to write:
Dear Whiffle, Blinky, Munch, and Mumbles,
As I sit here, on the morning of my last day on campus, I realize that there's no way I can just walk away without telling you how much you all mean to me. This year has been more than I could've ever imagined, and that's because of you.

From the very first time we met, you each brought your own unique magic into my life. Every adventure, every laugh, and every quiet moment has changed me. I'll carry all of it—and all of you—with me, no matter where I go.

Whiffle, my sparkly friend, you filled every day with laughter and light. From our glitter-filled burping contests to our midnight dance parties, you showed me how to find joy in the little things. You taught me that there's always room for a little more sparkle in life, and I promise, I'll never stop looking for it.

Blinky, you were my guide in every way. Whether it was lighting up a late-night study session or creating a magical glow in the middle of a crowd, you helped me find my way through every dark moment. Your light taught me that even when things seem impossible, there's always a way forward. Thank you for helping me find the light in myself.

Munch, my snack-loving buddy, you turned every moment into a celebration with your cookies, popcorn, and endless energy. You showed me that sometimes, a simple snack and a bit of humour are all you need to lift someone's spirits. Thanks to you, I'll always remember that life is better with a good snack and a lot of laughter.

Mumbles, you were my quiet, gentle friend, always there with a calming word or a wise whisper. You reminded me to slow down, to listen, and to appreciate the moments that often go unnoticed. Your calm presence taught me that sometimes, the softest voice holds the most wisdom. I'll carry that lesson with me always.

Each of you brought your own magic into my life, and together, you turned this year into a journey I'll treasure forever. I never would've imagined meeting friends like you—friends who could turn a simple study session into a night of laughter, who could make even the hardest days easier, and who would show me that magic truly exists, not just in glitter and glow, but in friendship and love.

Leaving you all behind feels like leaving a piece of myself. But as sad as it is, I know that I'm carrying you with me. Every laugh, every glitter trail, every glow in the dark... all of it is part of who I am now, because of you.

I hope that someday, I can bring a bit of the same magic into the lives of others. You've given me something beautiful—a belief in wonder, in adventure, and in the power of friendship. And I know that no matter where I go, that magic will be with me, guiding me and reminding me of everything we shared.

Thank you, my friends. For every adventure, every memory, and every moment. I'll never forget you, and I'll never stop being grateful for the year we spent together.

With all the love in the world,
Sammy

As he signed his name, Sammy's heart felt both heavy and light. It was hard to say goodbye, but he knew that this letter was a small piece of the magic he'd experienced—a reminder of the friendships that had changed him forever.

He folded the letter, placing it carefully on his desk where his friends would find it. As he stood up, he felt a familiar presence by his side, and he turned to see Whiffle, Blinky, Munch, and Mumbles, each one smiling, their eyes filled with understanding.

They didn't need words to say goodbye. They knew that this wasn't really the end, just the start of a new chapter.

One Last Embrace

Sammy hugged each of his friends, feeling the warmth of their magic, their laughter, and their friendship. Whiffle gave him a sprinkle of glitter for the road, Blinky gave a comforting glow, Munch tucked a cookie in his bag, and Mumbles offered a soft, reassuring whisper that echoed in his heart.

As Sammy walked out of his dorm room for the last time, he glanced back, seeing the faint shimmer of glitter and glow lingering in the air—a reminder of everything they'd shared.

The letter sat on the desk, a final tribute to the friends who'd taught him the true meaning of magic, and as he left campus, Sammy felt ready to face the world, knowing he'd always carry a piece of them with him, wherever he went.

And as he stepped forward, he knew one thing for certain: friendships like these, woven with magic and memories, never really end. They stay with you, shining softly, like a glow in the dark, lighting your path and reminding you of the wonders that life holds.

Chapter 29: The Surprise Return

Months had passed since Sammy's magical first year of college came to an end, and life had continued moving forward. He'd settled back into the familiar routine of home, adjusting to a quieter life without his monster friends by his side. Though he missed them deeply, he knew they were always with him in spirit—and in the little reminders he carried from their year together. The glowstone Blinky had given him sat on his desk, Whiffle's glitter vial was tucked safely in his backpack, Munch's cookie recipe was taped to the kitchen fridge, and Mumbles' magical compass was always in his pocket.

And now, graduation day had arrived. Sammy was proud, excited, and a little nervous as he prepared to cross the stage, officially closing the chapter on his first year. He'd made new friends and new memories, but nothing compared to those extraordinary months with Whiffle, Blinky, Munch, and Mumbles. As he stood among the sea of graduates, he wondered if they'd be proud of him, if they'd be cheering him on from wherever they were.

Little did he know, he wouldn't have to wonder for long.

The Surprise of a Lifetime

The ceremony was in full swing when Sammy's name was finally called. He stepped forward, feeling a surge of pride and excitement as he approached the stage. But just as he reached out to shake hands with the college dean, a faint, familiar sound caught his ear—a soft giggle, a whisper, and the unmistakable shimmer of glitter swirling in the air.

He glanced up, and there they were, right at the back of the auditorium: Whiffle, Blinky, Munch, and Mumbles, each one dressed up for the occasion in their own unique way, beaming at him with pride and joy.

Whiffle was decked out in a tiny graduation cap that sparkled with glitter, Blinky had tied a ribbon around himself that glowed faintly, Munch held up a sign that read "GO SAMMY!" in big, bold letters, and Mumbles was hovering quietly beside them, his smile soft and proud.

Sammy's eyes widened in disbelief, his heart racing with happiness. He grinned, resisting the urge to wave as he accepted his diploma. *They came,* he thought, his heart swelling. *They really came.*

The Monster Celebration

After the ceremony, as soon as the crowd began to disperse, Sammy made his way to the back of the auditorium, his smile widening with each step. As he reached his friends, they erupted into cheers, with Whiffle tossing glitter into the air and Blinky lighting up the entire area with a celebratory glow.

"Sammy!" Whiffle squealed, hugging him tightly and leaving a fresh dusting of glitter all over his graduation gown. "We couldn't miss your big day!"

Blinky hovered nearby, his glow steady and warm. "We're so proud of you, Sammy. This day is as much yours as it is ours."

Munch offered him a cookie, grinning. "A graduation cookie, specially baked just for you. You've earned it!"

Mumbles nodded, his voice a quiet whisper filled with pride. "We told you we'd always be with you. This is your moment, Sammy."

Sammy felt his eyes fill with tears as he hugged each of them, feeling a wave of love and gratitude. "Thank you. Thank you for being here… for everything."

A Magical Graduation Photo

As they celebrated, Whiffle had a mischievous idea. "Let's take a photo! You need a proper graduation picture—with all of us!"

They gathered around Sammy, who set his phone on a timer and placed it on a nearby bench. Just as the timer counted down, Whiffle sprinkled a handful of glitter, Blinky cast a soft glow, Munch held up his "GO SAMMY!" sign, and Mumbles created a gentle mist that swirled in the background.

The picture was perfect, capturing the magic of their friendship and the joy of the moment. Sammy knew it was a memory he'd treasure forever.

One Last Adventure on Campus

After the photo, his friends weren't quite ready to say goodbye. "One last tour?" Blinky suggested, his glow flickering with excitement.

Sammy laughed, nodding eagerly. "Let's go!"

They strolled through campus, revisiting all their favorite spots. They stopped by the fountain, where Whiffle sprinkled a final dusting of glitter, creating a magical glow over the water. They made their way to the library, where Blinky lit up their favorite reading nook one last time, casting a gentle warmth over the familiar space. Munch left a cookie on a table in the common room "for the next hungry soul," and Mumbles left a faint mist on the rooftop where they'd shared countless late-night talks.

Each stop was a tribute to their shared memories, a celebration of the magic they'd brought to each other's lives.

A Farewell Under the Stars

Finally, they returned to the lawn, where they lay in the grass under the stars, just like old times. The night was quiet, filled with the warmth of friendship and the bittersweet knowledge that their time together was coming to a close.

Whiffle took Sammy's hand, his voice soft. "We'll always be here, Sammy. Whenever you need us."

Blinky added, his glow flickering gently, "You carry our magic with you, even if you can't see us."

Munch handed him one last cookie, grinning. "And if you ever need a snack, remember, I'm with you in spirit."

Mumbles floated beside him, his voice barely more than a whisper. "Every star, every quiet night, every laugh... we're part of it all."

Sammy felt a tear slip down his cheek as he looked at each of them, his heart full. "Thank you. For everything. I'll never forget you."

They hugged him one last time, each friend wrapping him in their unique warmth, their magic, their love.

The Next Chapter

As the stars twinkled above, Sammy knew this wasn't really goodbye. His friends had given him the greatest gift of all—a belief in magic, in friendship, and in himself.

The next morning, Sammy woke up to find a small envelope on his pillow. Inside was a card that read:

"For Sammy, our friend and hero. May your life be filled with magic, adventure, and endless laughter. We'll always be with you, wherever you go."

And below it, in Whiffle's glittery handwriting, was a simple message: "You're never alone."

With a smile, Sammy tucked the card into his pocket, knowing that his friends—and their magic—would be with him every step of the way. No matter where life took him, he knew one thing for certain: the love of true friends, especially magical ones, was a gift that would last forever.

Disclaimer

This book is a work of fiction. The characters, events, and settings are purely the product of imagination. Any resemblance to real people, places, or actual events is entirely coincidental.

This book includes themes of friendship, adventure, and harmless pranks, all within a fantastical context. Please remember that the magical elements, including "invisible paint" and "glitter bomb parties," are imaginary. Always practice safety and respect others in real life, and consult an adult before recreating any activities or adventures inspired by this story.

Enjoy the magic responsibly, and have fun with Sammy and his monster friends!